In Just the Right Light

by

William R. Soldan

IN JUST THE RIGHT LIGHT
Copyright©2019 William R. Soldan
All Rights Reserved
Published by Unsolicited Press
Printed in the United States of America.
First Edition 2019.

This is a work of fiction. Names, characters, businesses, places, events, locales, and incidents are either the products of the author's imagination or used in a fictitious manner. Any resemblance to actual persons, living or dead, or actual events is purely coincidental.

Attention schools and businesses: for discounted copies on large orders, please contact the publisher directly.

For information contact:
Unsolicited Press
Portland, Oregon
www.unsolicitedpress.com
orders@unsolicitedpress.com
619-354-8005

Cover Design: Kathryn Miller
Editor: S.R Stewart ; Caitlin James

ISBN: 978-1-947021-85-3

In Just the Right Light

by

William R. Soldan

For Gabrielle, my mother

The eyes are not here
There are no eyes here
In this valley of dying stars
In this hollow valley
This broken jaw of our lost kingdoms

—T. S. Eliot, "The Hollow Men"

Table of Contents

Trapper's Creek

Late afternoon. The day was unseasonably warm, and for the second time since morning, he set out under a hazy smudge of blue-gray sky through woods ablaze with autumn fire. Nearby, a woodpecker hollowed out a home in a dying pine, the sound echoing down from the tree-lined ridge overlooking Miles Junction, a small town wedged in the jaw of northeast Ohio like an infected tooth. The kind of place where the air, depending on the way of the wind, carried on its back the rotten vapors of the local landfill or the sulfurous scent of the fish farm just over the state line. A place from which one could follow any point of the compass and discover remnants of a forgotten century: the vast quilt of bankrupt homesteads, fading tracts of corn and scrub unfolding in all directions; the Lornfield coal tipple and its aging brethren clinging to rocky slopes to the west; the chain of shuttered mills—Sharon Steel, Youngstown Sheet and Tube, Republic, and others—rusting on the banks of the poisoned river a short ride north; the last lonely freights running southbound rails toward the rugged heart of Appalachia; and the deep valleys to the east, each one its own quiet American tragedy.

In town, the last of the businesses—Kurtzal's Hardware, Mort's Little Shopper, and the only bar, Miller's Tap—continued to fight the good fight at the intersection of 67 and Main, despite the many that had long since surrendered. The Station Inn, The Butcher Block, the garages and auto shops, even the local elementary and high schools—all deserted. Windowless shells of crumbling brick, as if this section of the world had been used up, crushed and cast aside like an empty tin can left to molder in the high grass.

But for Arthur Pruitt, this was home. This small, forsaken place. Each day the earth reclaimed more and more, and soon it would be gone. It would all return to the dirt. But when that day came, he knew he'd no longer be here to see it.

#

He made the mile-long trek twice each day: just after dawn and a few hours before sunset, once he'd finished supper and deposited the bones of his nightly repast on the trash heap out back. His traps were hidden like landmines every hundred yards or so, starting at the buckthorn shrubs beside the cabin and going all the way back to the creek, which spewed from a drainage pipe a few miles north and eventually veered east toward Pennsylvania along the back edge of his property. Locals had long ago named the stagnant channel Trapper's Creek, on account of Arthur's blood. Generations of Pruitts had lived off this land. His pa and grandpap, both long dead, had taught him all he needed from an early age, and he'd hoped his only son would carry it on. But when Lester returned home after the fall of Saigon almost fifteen years ago, he'd been a haunted man in ways Arthur hadn't been prepared for. And when the stomach cancer took his mama not long after—well, there went hope.

Lester only got worse from then on, and now he spent his days with a head full of ghosts in the padded confines of Woodside Hospital over in Youngstown.

Though it was rare among folks these days, with the exception of going into town on occasion to get a few things—canned goods, fuel, tobacco, hardware supplies—Arthur subsisted largely on what nature provided. But ever since they'd found the boy's body the previous fall, he had done his best to avoid town whenever he could.

He'd received threats. He'd had his truck windows busted out, tires slashed, brake lines cut. Just this morning he'd come out of Kurtzal's, where he'd stopped for a box of nails, found *Killer* spray painted in red across his windshield. On the other side of the street, four men stood in the parking lot of Miller's Tap, leaning against a battered flatbed Ford, cigarettes stuck in their mouths. They glowered at him, eyes charged with burning hate, and something in their stares told Arthur that it wouldn't be long now.

He didn't know their names, but as he climbed behind the wheel of his pickup, one of them, a tall, rawboned man with a patchy beard and an East Lornfield Coal Co. cap on his head, said, "Better get that taken care of, Pruitt. You're liable to have an accident." The men all nodded slowly, the corners of their mouths downturned and their faces twisted behind the smoke from their cigarettes. As Arthur drove off, the same man who had spoken followed him with his stone gaze and ran a filthy thumb across his neck.

No, it wouldn't be long at all.

13

#

As he moved among the trees, breathing in the scent of dead leaves and damp earth, the air cloaked Arthur like a wet blanket. It was early October, yet the air was so muggy he could almost drink it down.

"If I don't drown by nightfall it'll be a goddamn miracle," he muttered to himself. The woodpecker's drumming stopped just then, as though waiting to see if the old man had more to say on the subject, then began again.

Most of his traps were small, coil-spring footholds. He had a few single- and double-door wire cages set up a little closer to the house, but he didn't rely on those much; critters tended to get wise to the cages, and besides, the footholds were easier to hide. When he was younger, he'd often used snares, but the years had taken their toll, and he could no longer work the knots. At sixty-five, his joints felt packed with sand and were as gnarled and knobby as the roots of a cottonwood.

Halfway to the water, Arthur had only a single squirrel tied to his belt. It had been dead when he found it, neck broken when the trap snapped shut. But now he came upon another, this one still alive, caught by the foot in one of the foot hold's jaws and gnawing itself to get free. As he watched the frantic creature, it brought back a memory of his son.

When Lester had come home from the service, something hadn't seemed right to Arthur, though he mostly brushed it off as his boy just needing to readjust; he was

14

distant, prone to wandering off and getting lost. Many nights Arthur would wake up to find Lester's bed empty and the front door swinging on its creaky hinges, and each time Arthur would grab a flashlight and go looking for him. Usually, he'd find Lester hunkered in some brush or behind a fallen log, eyes wide with visions only he could see. This went on for years, until Lester got himself caught one night.

It had been storming; rain fell so hard even the summer canopy offered little shelter. When Arthur finally discovered him, Lester's bare foot was clamped in one of the larger coil-springs. He was so out of his mind that he'd begun sawing his leg above the ankle with the bowie knife Arthur used to clean game, partially through the bone already and screaming, *They're all dead all dead all dead,* over and over. By the time Arthur got him home, got some tea and bourbon into him and bandaged him up with an old sheet, Lester's screams had ebbed into low moans that never quite stopped entirely, even as he slept.

That was the night Arthur accepted what he'd known to be true but had been denying since his son first came home: Lester was gone, his mind still in that goddamn jungle. What remained of him would have to be put someplace where there were people who could look after him properly.

He drove him to St. Elizabeth's in the city the following morning. The foot had festered too long, however, and they lopped it off before the infection spread. When Lester's body healed, Arthur signed the papers and had his boy committed. The decision was like a knife stuck in his guts, twisting a little more each time he thought about what he'd done.

He placed a boot on the squirrel's head, feeling it struggle as it sank into the soft dirt. He flexed his stiff fingers. Once they loosened up a little, he released the squirrel's mangled paw, gripped its scruff and body, and wrung its neck.

With images of his son still skimming the surface of his memory, Arthur continued toward the creek with the two squirrels hanging from his belt, their heads swiveling on broken necks and bobbing against his leg.

He came to the next trap, a foothold with a maw like a tiny shark. It was disengaged, but whatever had triggered it was long gone. He reset the spring and camouflaged it with some twigs and dead leaves.

Standing up, he massaged the small of his back, where wires of tightness had stitched themselves around his spine. He removed his faded red ball cap and ran a forearm across his sweaty brow. The woodpecker on the ridge had ceased its work for the time being, and the woods grew unnatural in their quiet. Despite his aching body and mind, Arthur let the stillness spread through him, and soon the self-loathing and despair he felt at the memory of his son became a dull remorse.

He stretched, placed the ball cap back on his head, and began moving again, this time through silence, save for the crunching of sticks and leaves beneath his boots. Ahead, the creek elbowed eastward through its stony groove, which separated the dense trees at the foot of the ridge from a wide field of creeping thistle, horseweed, and yellowing grass.

When he got to his final foothold, a large, toothy old thing, it was locked tight around a mangled possum. The animal was dead. It had been picked apart, its pelt in tatters, head attached by only a few strands of sinew and fur. *Damn*, he thought, and turned his eyes upward to see several dozen crows gathered in the treetops. They squawked and ruffled their feathers and hopped from branch to branch as they glared down at him.

He tossed the remains of the possum off to the side, reset the trap, and went to the water's edge to clean his hands. As the cool water sluiced through his fingers, Arthur felt the soft, muddy slope begin to give way under his feet. He backpedaled but not in time, letting out a raspy howl that echoed off the trees. He tumbled into the water and the serenity of the woods shattered into chaos as the crows began shrieking and flapping their wings.

The creek wasn't more than knee deep, but Arthur went under, arms flailing to catch his cap before the current carried it off. He got back to his feet, scrambled up the bank through a tangled mess of swamp rose, and made it back onto solid ground just as the slope once more threatened to slide out from under him. The crows' discord drew Arthur's eyes upward again, and he lost himself on a gnarl of roots, landing hard, twisting his ankle, and tearing a hole in the leg of his overalls. Though Arthur was a thin man, one of the

17

squirrels on his belt collapsed under his weight, the impact between his hip and a mossy rock crushing its ribcage. Fragments of angled bone poked through its pelt like broken teeth.

The crows continued their racket high in the trees. Arthur lay on his back looking up at the patches of October sky visible through the fiery leaves above. He was out of breath and dreading the walk back, so he closed his eyes, only for a moment, and tried to summon the will to stand.

#

There was a flutter of wings, like fabric whipping in the wind, as several crows grew bold and descended back to the forest floor to finish their meal.

Sleep had become a welcome prospect, and by the time his breath began to slow, Arthur had been close to drifting off. He likely would have, had it not been for the piercing pain of a beak pecking at his ankle, which had already begun to swell and bruise from the fall. A lone crow had broken away from the group, seeking fresher meat. He kicked the bird, shouted, "Git, you sonofabitch!" though there was little force behind the words. The bird retreated but lingered just out of reach, pacing from side to side.

Arthur mustered the energy to scoot himself up against a tree and placed his hand in something slick and warm on the ground beside him. He looked down; the broken squirrel's innards had leaked from its body onto the dirt. Wiping his hand across the wet thigh of his bibs, he removed a tobacco pouch and some matches from the breast pocket.

Soaked and useless. He threw them at the squawking bird, which stood its ground but soon lost interest in him and joined the others.

Watching the crows work on the possum, he thought about the dead boy again. They'd found him bound to one of the cottonwoods along the water. A hunter had spotted him through the scope of his rifle while tracking a deer along the base of the ridge. The photographs the police had spread out on the table in front of him the night the boy was discovered were of a life-sized ragdoll, pecked at and chewed on by birds and bugs. God knew what else.

"I didn't hurt no one," Arthur had said when they hauled him in for questioning. "I'm innocent."

He carried his own guilt about things. Everyone does. And he knew there were plenty of monsters in the world masquerading as men. But knowing it didn't make the idea that someone could do such a thing—to anyone, much less a child—any less difficult to reconcile.

"I never laid a hand on the boy," he said.

Sure, kids came nosing around on his property on occasion, rooting through his trash pile, but he'd only ever run them off with a shout or a shot in the air. No, the boy's death wasn't his burden to bear. But he knew such facts rarely mattered, not to those who needed someone to blame.

Arthur hadn't paid God much mind since his wife Betty passed, slowly and painfully, other than to spit His name out like spoiled meat. And he thought of Him even less after having to send his Lester away. But now, propped like a soggy burlap sack against the tree, Arthur found himself wondering about the human soul and if the spirit of that boy had moved on before or after the animals got to him.

This and similar thoughts played leapfrog in the cavern of Arthur's skull as his eyes again fell closed.

#

He woke up from a circus of fragmented words and shapes, wrenched from the depths by a jagged howl resounding through the woods. It was near dark, the trees black, hulking figures against the thickening purple sky.

How long had he been out? *Couldn't have been more than an hour or two*, he thought, judging by the fading light. The crows were gone, and the only remaining sounds were the soft babble of the creek and the rustling of small, unseen things.

And again—the howl.

He couldn't tell where it was coming from; it was a mile or so away but seemed to come from all sides.

He was stiff and slow moving on his sprained ankle, but still he navigated the darkness with a kind of tired grace. Hobbling toward home, he tried to sort through the scattered dreams from which he'd just emerged, images frayed at the edges and unraveling with each uneven step.

A faint residue remained. Cloudy snapshots. The same as they were every time he slept these days: pictures of the dead boy melting into pictures of *his* boy melting into other faces. The police, the public defender, the men . . . The clipped words and questions: *Why'd you do it? Have there been others?* The unexpected verdict: *Not Guilty.* The threats: *You're gonna burn in hell you sick sonofabitch! Gonna pay for what you done!*

These thoughts all merged into a mosaic of moments, spinning between his ears, breaking apart like fractured glass.

"Not your burden," he reminded himself, but it was no consolation.

The howl came through the trees again, and this time he placed it up ahead somewhere.

Toward home.

Soon the single howl became many. It was not a sound born of the woods, of coyotes or distant dogs, but of men. And as he neared the sound, neared home, the darkness began to lighten. The slender silhouettes of the trees sharpened against a warm orange glow. The voices returned then, *You're gonna burn . . . gonna pay . . . gonna burn!* They played on a continuous loop, and for a moment, Arthur thought perhaps he had never woken up. Perhaps he'd never fallen asleep. Maybe what was coming had come and gone.

But then he came to the tree line and smelled the smoke. Heard the fire crackling and spitting as it consumed his small cabin. His tool shed and truck, too, were both ablaze. A moment later, the truck's tires went. Then the gas tank, a shotgun blast booming off the surrounding hills.

21

Though something in his mind told him to stay where he was, within the seclusion of the trees, his instinct to save the only thing he had left was too strong. The fire was too hot, too high. It was all beyond saving, he knew. But before this reality could take root, before he could think twice, Arthur was standing in front of the cabin, staring into the hissing, hellish throat beyond the busted door.

The porch roof fell. Black smoke and fire spilled out from the broken windows, crawling up the side of the house toward the clear, star-strung sky. He turned when he heard a shuffling in the dark. Feet on gravel.

"Gonna pay for what you done," came the voice. Only this time it didn't come from inside his head. It came out muddied by liquor, first from one, and then from many. The heat burned against his back as he watched them, their eyes like hot coals as they moved out of the shadows and into the light of lapping flames.

Something Special

When I get to Dwight's, he's in his driveway cutting an old Crown Victoria in half with a propane torch. For as long as I can remember he's been going on about building himself a stretch limo by splitting a car in two and welding an extension in the middle. It looks like he's finally had enough of everyone down at Miller's Tap giving him shit about it.

There's a stereo tuned to a classic rock station and a speaker propped up in the living room window. A corrugated plastic awning slants from the side of the house, and under it sits Dwight's old man, Lefty, steeped in shade, wearing nothing but a pair of dirty cutoff shorts and sucking down an Old Milwaukee. His feet soak in a kiddy pool and several cans float around his ankles in the scummy water. "Hey, Hey, Jesse, what's the word?" he says, saluting me with his beer before draining the last of it and tossing the can in the pool with the others. He reaches into a Styrofoam cooler for another one, places it between his bare knees, and pauses to scratch the stump of his left arm. A crane accident at the mill years ago took it off just above the elbow. Hence the nickname.

"What's up, Lefty?"

There's a crack and a hiss as he pulls the tab of his beer, and foam runs over the top onto his legs, which are fish-belly pale.

"Stiff dicks and airplanes," he says. "But this damn thing's itchin' something fierce today. All these years and I still feel the sucker moving around. Thought they was just foolin' with all that phantom limb stuff, but sure as shit." He takes a few long swallows and spits a quick spurt onto his stump. "It's nothing a couple six or twelve more of these won't fix." He gulps from the can again, crushes it, and lets out a sudsy belch.

Dwight's focused on the flame of his torch. After finishing a cut across the roof, he removes the circular welding goggles he's wearing and rests them on his head. That's when he notices me. He shakes a Pall Mall from a pack he pulls from the back pocket of his Dickies, lights it with the welder, and chokes off the valve. "Gonna be a beaut when she's all done," he says, nodding toward the car.

"Uh-huh," I say.

"Guy I know over in Hillsville—traded him a pistol for it."

Rather than chit-chat, I get to the point. "Charlene's been on me about that hundred dollars," I say.

A couple months back, there was brief ray of hope that broke through the wall of mine and Charlene's dreary situation when I'd won the bid on a small remodeling job. Few weeks of steady labor. If we were lucky, it might get us above water long enough to brace ourselves for the next wave. But during a drunken lapse of judgment, I floated Dwight a hundred bucks after he gave me some song and dance about owing a bookie in the city and being a little

24

light. The next morning, I found him passed out behind the wheel of his truck in the side parking lot of Mort's Little Shopper, a litter of scratch-off lottery tickets covering his lap and strewn about the cab. I felt like a chump, but I never told him I knew what he'd done with the money.

When I finally told Charlene about it, she locked me out of the trailer for several days. It was February. At night I curled up in the backseat of my Olds, using a paint-spattered drop cloth I kept in the trunk as a blanket. I'd stare out the window and try to count the stars that were flung across the sky like broken glass, and sooner or later I'd fall asleep to the sound of my own chattering teeth.

"That right?" Dwight says. "She run out of other stuff to harp on you about, huh?"

"That's got nothing to do with it. Times are tough is all. You know that as good as anyone."

"Aw, I'm just bustin' your balls, brother. No need to get your panties all knotted up."

"So I guess you'll be squaring up, then?" I say.

He's silent for a moment, looks around at everything but my face. Finally, he says, "Well, I can't say I'm in the position to do that just now. But don't sweat it."

"'Don't sweat it'? Dammit, Dwight, you know I ain't working right now. You know I didn't have it to loan you in the first place, but I did because we go way back, and I was drunk and—"

I close my eyes and shake my head.

"I got something in the works," he says.

And here it comes, I think. The story. The scheme. I've known Dwight long enough to see it coming from a mile off.

"To hell with something," I say. "I need my money. We're scraping bottom. Government check's still two weeks away, and Charlene ain't bringing in nearly enough doin' makeovers and selling that Avon crap."

I stop talking for a moment and look over at Lefty, who's dozing in his chair under the awning, idly swatting at an enormous fly that keeps landing on his nose. Then I take a deep breath, tell myself it's either hear Dwight's big plan or never see that hundred dollars. And that's just not an option.

"It's a simple in-and-out type deal," he says. "Easy peasy."

I stare at him, motion for him to get on with it.

"There's a storage facility headin' over toward Middleton, you know the one?" he asks.

I nod.

"That guy I was working for, one just started up his own construction company? Fucker burned me on two weeks' pay. Tried to say the work was never finished. Anyway, I happen to know he's got a storage unit full of tools and equipment. I also happen to know there ain't shit for security. Had a unit there myself for a while. Damn place is wide open."

After thinking on it for a minute, I say, "Even if the gate's open, the unit won't be. Let's say I was on board. How you plan on gettin' in? Last I remember them places use disc-locks on the doors. Bolt cutters won't work, they're too thick, and there's no leverage. That's why they use 'em."

He picks up the welding torch, opens the gas valve, and ignites it with a flint striker. "Fire," he says. "It'll chop through one of those locks in no time."

"And I suppose you got somewhere to get rid of the stuff."

"I know a fella that'll take it off our hands," he says. "Split two ways, could be a nice chunk of cheese."

I consider it some more. Finally I ask, "When?"

"Figure we can go around twelve tonight," he says. "Should be quick."

As I continue thinking, he adjusts the torch, narrows the whipping flame into a tight blue point.

Lefty's emerged from his nap and is cursing the relentless fly still buzzing around his head. After draining the last of his second beer since I arrived, he stands, scratches his stump again, and staggers to a bush beside the house to take a leak.

"There ain't nothin' to lose," Dwight says, pulling the goggles back down over his eyes. The torch's flame burns like a wicked ember in each black lens. Without waiting for me to say yes or no, he returns his attention to the Crown Vic and begins working his way down the side.

There's always something to lose, so I say, "Speak for yourself."

But just then a Black Sabbath song comes on the radio, and he doesn't seem to hear me.

#

When I walk into the trailer, Charlene's on the couch in a pair of my boxer shorts and a tattered tube top that's beginning to unravel along the bottom. She's got the TV on and one of her Misty Menthols crammed between her lips, squinting against the smoke as she flips through the only three stations that come in.

Brendan's recently figured out how to remove the plastic safety covers on the wall sockets and is heading toward the one under the kitchen table when I catch him and stick him in his playpen.

"Babe, you really need to watch him better," I tell her. "He almost got at the outlet again."

"That bum pay you back our money?" she asks, her eyes glued to the screen. She settles on *Maury*, where a ratty looking asshole is jumping up and down on stage because the DNA test says he's not the father of some girl's kid.

"Not exactly."

She finally pries her eyes from the TV and looks at me. "What the hell's that supposed to mean?" she says.

"Got word on a job. Dwight says it should pull in enough to get back what I loaned him and then some."

She scoffs and jabs her skinny cigarette out in the ashtray. "Course he told you that. That sonofabitch's got more stories than a goddamn library."

"I know he does, baby, but what am I supposed to do? If he don't got it, he don't got it."

"Don't 'baby' me," she says. "What if he's blowin' smoke up your ass? Then what? I suppose you'll just let him go on owin' you. Meanwhile we ain't got a pot to piss in." I can see the muscles in her jaw working as she grinds her teeth.

I don't know what to say to her. She's right. If Dwight's little scheme doesn't pan out, if it all ends up being for nothing . . .

Finally, I say, "We can't afford for me not to take that chance."

"Damn right we can't," she says, her voice full of venom.

Brendan starts crying and Charlene gets up, grabs him out of his playpen. She props him on her hip and paces a few times between the towers of dollar-bin VHS tapes on either side of the old entertainment center, then goes and stands in front of the window fan. It's only late April, but the heat has already come down like a hammer. The fan lifts a few loose strands of her hair, which is wound up into a sloppy bun, and they float like straw-colored ribbons around her head. Her snake tattoo coils out from the fluttering fabric of my boxers and around her thigh.

When Brendan's crying doesn't let up, she grabs his bottle from the end table. Baby formula's another thing, a cost that pops up toward the middle of the month, after the food stamps and WIC vouchers run out.

"Gibson was by again," she says. "Wants the last two months' rent by the beginning of next week or we're gonna be pitching a tent in the woods." She walks to the kitchen counter and picks up a stack of mail. "And there's these." She throws the stack at my feet. The bills lay fanned out on the floor, and the words *Final Notice* come at me from different angles. They break past my eyes and knock around inside my skull like wasps in a jar. In addition to the food assistance we get, there's the little bit of TANF money on the first, but it never gets us out of the hole—it's just too deep. A wedge of sunlight creeps its way across the linoleum and I suddenly feel smaller than the specks of dust stirring inside it.

"If you don't take care of this," she says, "I'm gonna start dancin' again. Don't test me. Rico said he'd hire me back. All I gotta do is make the call."

Every time we're in a pinch, which seems like all the time lately, Charlene threatens to go back to stripping. She could do it, too; she's held up real nice. Her refusal to ruin her tits breastfeeding, even though it's supposed to be better for the baby and would save us a few bucks, might have something to do with it. She seems to think so.

She thrusts Brendan at me, snatches her cigarettes from the table, and stomps toward the bedroom at the back of the trailer. She shouts, "And your son needs diapers, if you even care," then slams the bedroom door. The sound starts Brendan crying again, so I hug him and tell him everything will be okay.

#

I first met Charlene when she was stripping at a place called Mustang Sally's, over by the Penn-Ohio truck stop where I was working as a diesel mechanic.

I was sitting in the restaurant one evening after busting my knuckles under the hood of a Peterbilt for ten straight hours when I saw her standing outside the club across the lot. It looked like she was waiting on a ride. It was winter, and she had on this gaudy coat with sparkly studs, fishnets, and a skirt that barely qualified. She had a big purse slung over her shoulder and her knee-high leather boots caught the light from the fueling station.

After I finished my coffee, I got in my car and swung around to the side of the lot where she was standing on the curb.

"Cold out here," I said, the heater in my Olds knocking as the engine warmed up. Her dark blonde hair was a mass of rolling waves, and I could tell that even underneath the smoky eyeshadow and blood-red lipstick she had a face that could stop traffic.

"My ride's just runnin' late," she said, keeping her eyes trained on the far end of the lot and the entrance from the highway.

"About forty-five minutes late by my watch," I said.

She turned toward me, a look of nervous disgust on her face. "You been watchin' me, you perv?"

"No . . . well, yes . . . I mean, I was in the restaurant across the way, saw you standing there."

She looked away again, ignoring me when I offered her a lift. I was about to offer again when she said, "I ain't for sale, if that's what you're thinking."

I wasn't looking to get in her pants, I told her, and even if I was, I'd never paid for it and wasn't about to start now. Then I realized that I might have sounded like a creep and said, "I didn't mean—"

"I know what you meant, Stud, and I ain't interested."

I told her I'd be happy to let her stand out there and freeze, or to wait for some sleazebag in the club to come out and make her a less honorable offer, but she just went on watching for her ride.

"Suit yourself," I said and rolled up my window.

I waited for another minute, and when I finally put the car in gear and began pulling away, she yelled, "Hey, wait."

I heard the faint clacking of her boot heels as she moved delicately around the car like a tightrope walker, trying not to slip on the icy pavement. When she got in, I could smell her perfume mixing with the scent of diesel exhaust. One of her clear stripper pumps and something feathery like a scarf poked out from the top of her big purse. The vents in the car's dash had finally begun to breathe warm air. She held her hands out and rubbed them together.

As she sat there, trying to get warm, I glanced down at the intricate scales of the snake coiled around her left leg, faintly visible through her stockings. She saw me staring at it. "Girl in this line of work's gotta have something special to set her apart," she said. "This is my something special."

By the time we got to the apartment she shared with the roommate who left her standing in the cold, I'd learned that she had started stripping to save up enough for cosmetology school. But after getting her certificate, she realized she could make more dancing in one night than she could making ugly people look good for a living. Especially around here. "A makeup artist ain't in very high demand in northeast Ohio," she said. So she promised herself that someday she'd head out to L.A., maybe New York City. "But for now, I'm just gonna keep dancing. I'm good at it."

Things happened pretty fast after that. We went out a few times, she had a falling out with her roommate, and before long she'd moved into my trailer.

I never went to see her dance at the club, but one night in the living room she gave me my own private show. She used a standing lamp as a prop, and I found out just how good she was.

Her rattlesnake tattoo was much bigger than I had thought the first night we met and shaded in a way that made it look real. The rattle sat on the back of her thigh just above the knee, and the snake wrapped itself around her left leg. From there it worked its way around her torso, under her breasts, over her shoulder and down her right arm, its spade-shaped head resting in the crook of her elbow, flicking its forked tongue. She had this way of moving. It brought the snake to life, like it might strike if you got too close.

#

Charlene hasn't come out of the back bedroom all afternoon, except to feed the baby. I'm out of cigarettes, so I roll one with a Zig-Zag and some butts from the ashtray while I watch Brendan play with one of the plastic half-gallon vodka bottles he's managed to drag from the bin by the door. He only started crawling a few weeks ago, but since then he's been on the move and into everything.

When we found out Charlene was pregnant, we both agreed to keep the baby. And no matter how hard things get, scraping by, barely able to keep the power on some months, I don't regret our decision. I love the little guy like I've never loved anyone or anything in my whole miserable life. Sometimes, thinking about the way he babbles and drools, how his big eyes are always filled with wonder about everything—sometimes that's the only thing that gets me through the day.

Before he was born, I wouldn't have been quite so hesitant to do a job with Dwight. It was never something that needed much considering. But as I see Brendan there on the discolored carpet in the middle of the living room, I remind myself that things aren't quite so simple anymore, that I need to take him into account before jumping to do something that could land me in jail. Or worse.

I'm on the verge of calling Dwight and telling him to forget it. I have a family to think about. Find someone else to help you and let me know when you've got my money. I have the receiver in my hand.

But then, that very idea—that I have a family to think about—becomes razor sharp in my mind when I see the diaper Brendan's wearing, fastened with duct tape because he's out grown the size-threes we got at the charity drive over at St. John's. He's too little to know any better, but the sight of it is enough to make me want to cry or punch a hole through the wall. I remember the time we didn't have any diapers at all and had to fashion one out of a dishtowel and some of Charlene's panty liners that she keeps around for emergencies.

That's what seals it.

I hang up the phone.

Brendan grows bored with the plastic bottle. He crawls over to the bag of garbage beside the stove in the kitchen and starts chewing on a discarded cereal box. I take one last hit from my rolled cigarette, crush the cherry between my fingers, and flick it into the sink. Then I scoop Brendan up

35

off the dirty linoleum and take him back into the living room where I sit with him on the floor in front of the TV, redirecting him every few seconds when he starts heading for something he shouldn't. I give him back the empty vodka bottle to play with. He really seems to like that thing, and I'm not sure how to feel about that.

#

Dwight picks me up in his truck around 11:30, and we head out to the storage facility about a quarter mile from the Middleton line. Just before it comes into sight, Dwight pulls over to the shoulder of the road and jumps out to remove the truck's plates.

"Just in case," he says. "Ain't no security cameras, but you never know where there's eyes."

The place sits back from the road, down a slight slope at the end of a gravel drive. The chain link that surrounds it is topped with kinky lengths of barbed wire, and at each corner of the perimeter stands a towering vapor lamp, three of which are burned out. The one remaining spotlight hovers like a UFO, casting its electric beam from high in one of the front corners and leaving the back half of the place shrouded in darkness.

The gate isn't even latched, and I wait in the truck while Dwight slides it open on its squeaky track.

He waves me forward, so I scoot over behind the wheel and drive through. Dwight hops in the passenger side.

"Straight ahead," he says. "Around back."

36

The facility is, at most, only a few hundred units. Four long rows of identical lockers with roll-up doors run from front to back, with a fifth row that runs along the backside. Each unit has its own little light fixture, but most are fried or missing their bulbs.

As we make our way between two of the long structures toward the back, gravel crunches beneath the tires like old bones, and the cab of the truck suddenly feels too warm and stuffy. I'm struggling to breathe. I try telling myself it's just adrenaline, but it doesn't help. I hang my head out the window, but the night air is syrupy in my lungs, and the scent of a nearby cow pasture is so intense I can taste it in the back of my throat. With each passing second, I'm becoming more aware of the literal shit I'll be trudging through if things get hairy and I have to run.

I turn right when we get to the end of the row, then make two successive lefts until we're on the backside of the facility, which faces a fence and acres of dense, shadowy trees.

"Stop here," Dwight says. "Turn her around. Worse comes to worse, we're goin' full bore through there." He points out the rear window at the section of chain link separating us from a shallow gully and a dirt access road on the far rise, which leads to a limestone quarry in one direction and connects with the main highway in the other.

He jumps out and starts walking toward the other end, shining a small flashlight above the doors until he finds the one he's looking for. By the time I get the pick-up turned around, he's back and grabbing his welding gear from the bed of the truck.

"All right," he says. "Alls I need you to do is stand at that corner and keep lookout, holler if you spot trouble."

I walk over. From the corner, I have a clear view of the highway and the drive leading back to the gate. Making a circle with my thumb and index finger, I flash him the OK sign.

Less than a minute later I see sparks.

I made decent money at the garage. We wouldn't be trotting off to the Bahamas anytime soon, but it was enough to pay the bills, sock a little away each week, and even have a night out once in a while. Although I was never one to interfere with people capitalizing on their talents, I began having trouble with Charlene's career alternative, and tried convincing her that she should hang up her heels. I told her I'd take care of her, that someday soon I'd take her far away from this place if that's what she really wanted.

She seemed hesitant to rely on such promises, but she eventually agreed.

Six months later we were hitched, and just as quick she was pregnant with Brendan. Charlene had grown up in foster care, and my folks had divorced shortly before Pancreatitis killed my old man and my mom moved off to Montana with her new boyfriend. So the thought of starting a family was something that seemed to bring me and Charlene even closer for a time.

We were happy.

Then one day, my boss, Marvin, told me he had to let me go. He had a nephew—his only sister's boy—who'd just been released from the Lucasville Pen and needed the job to satisfy the terms of his parole.

I'd never minded the man, even considered him good people, but as he stood there in his clean Dickies, with his clean hands and not a spot of grease on him, I realized we were different breeds. "Don't think that's legal, Marv," I said.

"How's that?" he asked, though the look on his face told me he knew exactly what I meant.

"Pretty sure you can't just fire a man with no warning, for no reason."

He put his hands in his pockets and looked thoughtfully at the ground. "You know, Jesse, you're a good worker. But family's family. You understand."

"And what about mine," I said.

He wouldn't look me in the eye. "I'm sorry, but like I said."

"Suppose I take you to court, then."

That's when he looked up. His face, which had seemed somewhat sympathetic, was now cold and rigid. "Now don't go makin' this harder than it's gotta be," he said. "But if that's how you want it."

I stared him down, trying to appear like I hadn't already given up. But lawyers cost money. Good ones, anyway. And that was something I no longer had. I threw an oily shop rag at the ground, and it landed on the toe of one of his spotless Red Wings.

Sitting in the car, I was suddenly no different from all those sorry schmucks wandering around like lost dogs when the steel mills closed, low on skills and too stunned to know what the hell to do next. Odd jobs hanging drywall and the occasional engine repair brought in a little. But it was never enough.

Charlene right away said she'd go back to Mustang Sally's after Brendan was born if I wanted her to, but I refused to let my wife shake her ass for truckers and dirtball tweakers just because I'd failed to deliver on my promises. We'd manage somehow, I told her. But by the time little Brendan popped out, I'd already begun writing bad checks just to get gas and pay for the cheap vodka that helped dull the reality of every dragging day without work. Charlene did makeovers for girls going to homecoming and prom, and started selling cosmetics from the Avon catalogue to the girls' mothers. But for all the ugly people out there looking to conceal their genetic misfortunes, there were never enough of those either.

#

It takes Dwight less than a couple minutes to cut through the lock, but it might as well be days. Standing at the corner unit, watching the road, I'm getting antsy, shifting my weight from foot to foot and clenching my fists so tight my fingernails dig into my palms. My stomach's queasy and my mouth is dry.

I spot a car on the main road that I think is slowing down, but it turns out to be just a Jeep with its top off full of drunken teenagers, hooting and howling and hanging out the back.

They pass and I begin thinking about what the current mandatory sentences might be for the multiple laws we're violating:

Trespassing.

Breaking and entering.

Burglary.

Destruction of private property.

Probably others.

I wonder if the judge will run the sentences concurrent or consecutive.

On top of my already-throbbing nerves, it feels as if gravity itself just increased and is pressing me into the rocky ground.

I snap out of my paralysis when I hear Dwight lift the locker door. A moment later he flips a switch inside and a square of light spills across the gravel and the tall grass on the other side of the fence.

I'm still watching the road, but it's as dark and still as the woods behind me.

Dwight peeks his head out and gives a little whistle. "Back the truck up here," he yells in a whisper.

When I back up in front of the door, he starts tossing bags and boxes and drill cases into the bed. He's hoisting a miter block over the side when he says, "Jump out and help me load up that table saw and air compressor."

We clean the place out in about as much time as it took to get in. When we're finished, Dwight kills the light, closes the door, and chucks the mangled lock toward the trees.

I slide back into the passenger seat and let him drive us out. He keeps the headlights off until we're back on the road. I watch the facility shrink from sight in the side-view mirror, and when it's just darkness back there Dwight pulls over to put the plates back on. While he's squatted down in front, oncoming headlights crest a hill ahead of us.

It's the drunken teenagers again. As they motor by one of them is standing in the back, holding onto the roll bars and screaming something about being totally wasted as the others cheer him on. Their voices are swallowed by the night and the Jeep's taillights look like red eyes. When Dwight pulls back onto the highway, I steal one more look from the side view mirror as the Jeep makes a reckless turn onto the access road leading back to the quarry.

"Nutty kids," Dwight says as he gets back in the truck. "Sure takes you back, though, don't it?"

"Sure does," I say, and half wonder how long it will be before someone finds the bloody wreckage.

#

In the morning, Dwight off-loads every tool and bit of equipment we stole to a guy he knows in Newcastle, PA, right across the state line. Easily ten-grand-worth of gear brings us half that. Split both ways and I walk away with twenty-five hundred, which is more cash than I've held in my hands in a long time.

"Told you, brother," Dwight says, handing me my cut. "Easy peasy."

It's hard to believe we pulled it off. I keep folding the money, putting it in my pocket and taking it out again, counting it, feeling the texture of the paper. I have to assure myself it's real, that I'm not just having one of those wonderful dreams, the kind that turns out to be a cruel nightmare when its sweetness is obliterated by the sound of your alarm clock and you're violently reeled back into a state of unfortunate awareness.

Dwight stops in at Mort's for a pack of smokes and some scratch-offs. "What's say we hit the Tap, knock back a few," he says when he comes out of the store.

I consider it for a moment, but decide I better go home instead. "Think I'll get back to Charlene and the baby, if I know what's good for me," I say. "I should let her know she can stop hating me—at least for a while." I let out the strained laugh of someone who knows all too well that he's come close to losing all that matters to him, but who's miraculously acquired the means to keep such an outcome at bay, if only for a short time.

#

The first thing I do when Dwight drops me back at the trailer is walk up the hill to Gibson's house. He opens the door wearing a faded pair of Carhartt overalls and a baseball cap sitting crooked on his fat head. He's got a plug of chew in his cheek and a pouch of Beechnut sticking out of his breast pocket, and when he smiles at me his teeth are mossy and brown.

I pull out the fold of bills, peel off nine-hundred and hand it to him. "For this month and the last two," I say.

He spits a thick string of tobacco juice over the porch rail where it catches on a withered rose bush, hangs there for a moment, and falls to the ground. "You know, I don't like having to come knockin' every time rent's due, son," he says, folding the cash and stuffing it in his overalls.

"It might be a little late," I say, "but I always pay what I owe. I ain't never done you wrong in that regard."

"True you haven't. But that don't mean I won't put you out if it happens again, you hear?"

I nod and walk back to the bottom of the trailer park, leaving him to chomp his chaw like a cow in a field. On my way down the hill, I think about how a greasy sonofabitch like Gibson can have such sway over my circumstances, and I'm amazed that I've made it this far without eating the barrel of a gun.

#

After paying the rest of the overdue utilities and getting Brendan some diapers that actually fit, we hit the food bank for our monthly handout. We get some canned goods, bread, peanut butter, a box of rice and beans, and some other items. It should be about two weeks before we're back to rationing the Ramen noodles.

Charlene gets her friend Trish to watch Brendan for the evening while we go into town and tie one on at the Tap. Of course, we shouldn't piss money away at the bar, but sometimes you convince yourself that, by God, you've earned a little reprieve.

After last call, we go back to the trailer and Charlene dances for me just like she used to. Then we fuck for the first time in months.

"I love you, baby," she says as she kisses my chest, then spins herself around. She throws her head back. I smack her behind, and the sweaty tips of her hair stick to her skin. I squeeze her hips as she works them on top of me. She moans and says it again: "I love you, baby," but part of me knows it's just the liquor talking.

#

Three weeks pass. We're down to our last two-hundred bucks, and a new month is lurking right around the corner.

45

The good thing is we'll be getting our food stamps soon. Meanwhile, though, the cupboards are bare and Brendan's got a temperature. He's been shrieking until his face turns purple, and he's covered in snot and tears. He keeps batting at the side of his head and pulling on his earlobes. I want to wave my hand over him, make his pain disappear, and I feel utterly helpless because I can't.

I'm looking for some clean clothes to put on him, but my head is reeling and everything is dirty. Charlene's trying desperately to comfort him. She rocks him gently and hums a soft tune.

"Hurry up," she tells me.

"Put this on him," I say, tossing her a striped onesie with a stain on it. I stuff a couple toys and the last two diapers in a bag and pace around the living room while she gets him dressed.

He settles down long enough for us to get him into the car, but before we're even on the road to the hospital he's screaming bloody murder again.

Charlene sits in the back with Brendan and doesn't say a word to me the entire ride.

Once we're there, the doctor, a clean-shaven man with a white coat and a clipboard, informs us that Brendan has an infection in both ears and gives him a shot of antibiotics. All the while he talks in a condescending tone and gives us that look of pity and veiled contempt reserved for shelter winos and folks on welfare. Then he writes us a scrip and says it should start to clear up within a few days.

"In the meantime," he says, "give him baby aspirin for the pain and fever. And schedule a follow up with your pediatrician as soon as possible." He pauses. "You *do* have a pediatrician?"

"Of course, Doc," I say. "What do you take us for?"

He looks skeptical, but before I can say anything else, he's out the door.

We pick up some food after we leave the pharmacy and have just enough left for more diapers and formula, gas, smokes, and a bottle of Aristocrat.

When we get home, it's almost dark and Charlene still hasn't spoken to me. She feeds Brendan until he finally falls asleep, then hands him to me and grabs her purse and the car keys off the table.

"Where you goin'?" I ask her.

"Out for a bit," is all she says.

She has her hand on the doorknob and I say, "Char, wait." But she doesn't turn to face me.

"Just need to clear my head," she says before walking out the door.

I peek through the window blinds and briefly her face appears in the darkness of the Olds as she lights a cigarette.

Then she's gone.

After a couple hours I doze off on the couch still holding Brendan in my arms.

Around 2 a.m., I wake up to the sound of keys hitting the table and some infomercial flashing across the TV screen.

"Char?" I say, rubbing my eyes into focus.

She doesn't answer, just heads back toward the bedroom, listing from side to side against the walls of the narrow hallway.

#

On my way to the plasma center I pass by Dwight and Lefty's, where they're stomping cans in the garage and filling a garbage bag. There are several more bags piled in the back of Dwight's truck. I tap the horn twice and Lefty gives me a wave with his good arm. When they're finished, they'll drive over to the recycling plant and get themselves enough for a twelve-pack. Hardly seems worth the trouble, but then, neither does much else these days.

Dwight's project—the stretch limo—sits in two pieces in the driveway, propped up by bottle-jacks and covered with sheets of plastic, forgotten. Most likely he'll get me to help him haul it to the scrap yard. He'll toss me a few bucks for my time and then go on one of his scratch-off benders while he waits for Lefty to get his disability check. Who knows, maybe he'll hit it big.

#

They siphon thirty dollars-worth of plasma from my arm, give me two crisp bills, and send me on my way with a shot of orange juice and a stale chocolate chip cookie.

I'm still light-headed when I get to the truck stop by the turnpike, but I enjoy the feeling so instead of eating lunch I just get a cup of coffee. I think there are still a few squares of Ramen at home and tell myself that later I'll pick up a few cans of tomato soup, whip up something resembling spaghetti.

Three cups of sugary black coffee later, my gut turns on me, and I barely make it to the john in time after paying the check.

My head is swimming and the acidity of the coffee feels like it's eating a hole right through me. I hope it's not an ulcer.

Sitting on the can, I look over the graffiti on the stall door: penises and swastikas; snippets of profane verse concerning redheads, trailer hitches, and some guy named Roy who diddles little boys; phone numbers promising good times. It makes my head hurt.

As I'm doing up my pants, I hear two voices enter the restroom.

"Boy oh boy," one of them says. "You see how she made that snake shake its rattle?"

"Oh, I got me a real good look at that one," says the other.

I stand motionless.

"Don't know if I've *ever* seen an ass move like that. Girl's got talent."

I flush and exit the stall.

One man is pissing in a urinal while the other stands at the sink picking his teeth with the edge of a matchbook. They both go silent as I approach to wash my hands, and the one beside me gives me a dumb open-mouthed look in the mirror.

I'm facing the opposite wall, about to hit the button for the hand dryer when one of them says to me, "What do you think, pal?"

I glance over my shoulder.

"You ever see the little hottie with the snake across the way?"

"Yeah," I say, "She's something special, all right." One of my wet hands is clutching the keys in my pocket, and I wonder how many times I could stab him in the neck or the eye before his friend overpowers me.

I punch the button instead.

When I'm done drying my hands and turn around, they grin at me and nod, as if now we're all friends.

As they're walking out the door, I say, "Hey, fellas."

One turns first, and I catch him square in the nose with my fist, but before I can land another blow the other guy, a

50

real corn-fed country motherfucker, bull rushes me into the back wall. My head smacks the tile and I see spots explode in front of my eyes. When I look up, there are two bodies moving in over me. The one I decked holds a hand to his face and blood leaks through his fingers. His buddy looks eager, like knocking the hell out of someone is something he's been looking forward to all day.

Then come the steel-toed kicks to the body, the ragged knuckles to the face.

They take the twenty-eight dollars I have left in my wallet and leave me in a stall, piled between the toilet and metal divider like a heap of old rags. I don't think any bones are broken, but I can already feel my eye swelling shut and lumps forming above my hairline and on the back of my head where it hit the wall. Resting my face against the cold, dirty metal, I think of Brendan and wonder where he is.

#

I find a quarter in the cup holder of the Olds and call home. Trish answers, says she's watching Brendan while Charlene's out. She borrowed Trish's car for the day with a promise to fill the tank. She also told her she'd throw in some smokes and few extra bucks, which satisfied Trish enough to not ask where Charlene was going or how long she'd be gone.

But I don't need her to tell me.

I hang up the phone, and the force of the sun as I cross the lot makes me sweat. It runs down my face, stings in the cuts around my eyes, and mixes with the metallic taste of coagulating blood on my lips.

When I stagger in the front door, into the entryway of Mustang Sally's, I'm greeted by a mammoth skinhead with no neck and a mean face. He stands with his arms folded, stock still and as wide as a phone booth.

"The fuck happened to you?" he asks, his flat expression never changing.

"Bumped into a wall," I say.

"It's a five-dollar cover," he tells me.

I reach for my money but then remember it's gone.

"I'm broke," I say.

"Can't pay, can't stay," he says, still not moving his position.

Some asshole walks in behind me and starts griping for me to hurry up or get out of the way. The skinhead waves him forward, takes his money and lets him through.

I try to push past as the door opens, but the bouncer shoves me back with a meaty palm to the chest. "Don't even think about it, buddy," he says.

My eyes haven't yet swelled completely shut, and when I look inside, she's at the far side of the dark bar, on stage. Colored lights flicker and strobe above her as she flips and twists and grinds on the pole. She struts to the edge of the lit-up runway like she owns the place and drops herself into a split. A shadowy arm reaches out of the front row and stuffs a bill in her mouth, which she removes, folds and tucks in her G-string. Then she crawls back to the pole like a cat, circles it twice and climbs her way up it, hand over hand, until she's on her feet.

I try to scoot past the bouncer again, but this time he gets me in a bear hug and cuts off my air.

I don't struggle for long.

But before I lose sight of her, I watch the snake come to life one more time. Then the music fades, and everything else, as the door swings closed between us.

The Call

What is it this time? This was the first thought that entered Louis Beckett's mind. He had just finished clearing the snow and ice from the windshield of his brand new '78 Bronco and climbed behind the wheel, when officer Ritz came out of the station to tell him about the call. His second thought was that he ought to let this one alone. It was a thought that returned to him time and again over the years, and it always came on the heels of a name: Nancy Foster.

"She asked for you specific, Chief."

"Don't suppose she said what it's about?" Beckett said.

"Just that it was urgent," Ritz said. "Told her you'd already gone for the night, but she said she'd only speak to you. Then she hung up. Saw you was still here and thought you'd wanna know."

Ritz stood in the cold, no coat on, rubbing his arms for warmth.

"Well, I suppose it can wait till tomorrow," Beckett said. "Now go on and get back inside, son."

"And if she calls back?"

"She won't." He knew she wouldn't—at least, not tonight. "But if she does, you call me at home."

"Sure thing, Chief." At that, Ritz nodded and hurried back into the station.

Beckett sat in the driver's seat for several minutes, listening to the engine idle and wondering what the hell she'd gotten herself into. Had to be something. She only called when there was trouble.

"And it's no one's fault but your own," he said to his reflection in the rearview mirror.

He'd started down this path with her damn near twenty years ago, back when he was still just an officer. A call had come in late one Saturday night—an altercation at Miller's Tap. When he'd arrived, a young Nancy Foster was three sheets to the breeze and waving a broken beer bottle at a woman who'd confronted her for flirting with her husband, while about eight others stood around gawking. He'd managed to diffuse the situation peaceably and convince the other woman not to press charges. He told himself then it was because he hadn't wanted to deal with the paperwork and cause her a bunch of legal trouble she likely couldn't afford. But it had been more than that. He'd been attracted to her. Purely a physical thing. Her dark hair, piled on her head, sleeveless white blouse, and black jeans snug against a pinup figure. He'd only recently moved back after spending the last few years as a city cop in Youngstown, and he was alone, a man with urges like any other. He put Nancy in the back of his cruiser and took her home to sleep it off. And when he walked her to her door and she invited him in for a drink, he knew better. But his desire overpowered his good sense. That night he shared her bed. And such seemed to be the course of things every time thereafter. She'd get herself in a bind, and he'd come running. Since that first night, he'd gotten her out of D.U.I.s and hit-and-runs, handled domestic disputes, and paid off debts. He'd even neglected to file reports that would have landed her in court or jail on more than one occasion. Never learned.

"Goddamn fool is what you are," he told himself now.

He examined his features for a moment. Christ, he was looking old. Bunched up beneath his hat and above the lined collar of his coat, his exposed face was a harrowed terrain of deep creases and fractured lines. Worse yet, he was starting to *feel* old. Too old to keep getting reeled back in.

But that, he knew, was exactly what was about to happen.

#

When he got home, Beckett changed out of his uniform and turned on the radio, scanning through a number of stations playing Motown and disco hits until he landed on Bob Seger and the Silver Bullet Band. Then he popped a can of Stroh's, relaxed in his chair, and contemplated whether to pick up the phone.

"What do you think?" he asked. Boomer, his old German Shepherd, looked up from his spot on the floor beside him. "Should we call her?"

As if refusing to be a part of this decision, Boomer got up and trotted off to the toilet for a drink of water.

"Some friend you are," Beckett said.

He thought about it for a few more minutes as he finished his beer, but finally accepted that he was always going to call, and that he might as well quit pussy-footing around it. So he went into the kitchen and dialed her number.

The extension rang and rang. But by the time he counted a dozen and still no answer, he hung up and grabbed another beer from the fridge. The wind howled outside, and he stood for a moment, looking through the window at his back yard and the frozen hills beyond. Under the cold January moon, smoke drifted from distant chimneys, and a small cluster of deer moved across a neighboring field to the east. The countryside was a barren white waste, yet between songs, the radio in the other room was calling for even more snow over the next few days.

He was about to return to his chair in the living room when the phone rang, startling him a little. He picked up the receiver.

"It's me," she said.

"Figured it might be," he said, lifting his beer to his lips. "I just tried to call."

"I was out."

Silence followed. A beat, then two.

"Well," he said, "what's the problem?"

She released an exasperated breath into his ear. "It's that damn girl again. Run off somewhere."

Her daughter, Missy. Last couple years she'd been acting out, getting into things.

"You two fightin' again?"

"She's probably shacked up with some boy, you ask me."

"I am askin' you."

More silence. Then: "I got a call from the school today. Says she ain't been there in a week."

"And, what'd you say?"

"Told 'em she was home with the flu. Then that bitch secretary said if I don't provide a document verifying she's sick, they're gonna have to report it."

"So what exactly you think I'm supposed to do about it?" Beckett asked.

"Hell, never mind," she said. "If I knew it was gonna be a goddamn bother I wouldn't have called."

"No?"

"Like I said, forget it."

"Calm down," he said. "Did I say it was a bother?"

"I don't know, did you?"

"Look, I'll come over and we can figure this out."

"No," she said. "Now's not a good time."

"You got someone there with you?"

"That's none of your business," she said, which was all the answer he needed.

He flushed with a jealous anger, but kept it from coloring his voice. "Missy's sixteen years old. Like you said, she's probably with a boyfriend. I'm sure she'll be back around tonight."

"If she ain't?"

"Then I'll see what I can do." He downed the last of his beer, and somewhere in the background on her end, he heard music start playing. "Now go on," he said. "You don't want to keep your company waiting."

He hung up before she could respond.

Prior to her calling, Beckett had been thinking about fixing some supper, but he no longer had an appetite. He took the remainder of the twelve-pack from the fridge and returned with it to his chair, where, for the next couple hours, he burned his way through a pack of Pall Malls and drained the cans one by one.

#

"Mornin,' Lou," said Cathy when Beckett walked in the next day, bundled in his thermal coat and fur-lined hat.

"Mornin,' Cath." He kicked the snow from his boots on the rubber mat. Then he asked, "Coffee?"

"Just put on a fresh pot."

"I'll tell ya, temperatures don't go back up soon, these old bones might not make it much longer," he said, and breathed into his cupped hands.

"Please," Cathy said, "fifty-two is hardly old. Complain to me in another ten or fifteen years."

Cathy was sixty-four-years-young, she liked to say, and never failed to give Beckett a hard time when he started griping about his age. She had carpal tunnel in both wrists *and* a mean set of bunions, she reminded him, and still made her husband, Harold, an old-fashioned breakfast of biscuits and gravy every morning before tidying up and coming to work. "You men wouldn't make it a week without a woman to look after you," she told him nearly every day. Then she'd invariably smile and say it was a wonder he put his shoes on the right feet without a wife to give him instructions.

"Any calls?" Beckett asked, pulling the lever on the stainless-steel coffee urn and filling his cup.

"A Nancy Foster," she said, looking down at her message pad. "Asked for you."

Beckett sipped his coffee, let the warmth work its way through him. He hoped she'd only called to let him know Missy had come home sometime in the night. But he suspected it was the opposite. Rather than let Cathy start wondering why he had it memorized, he accepted the slip of paper with Nancy Foster's phone number on it when she held it out to him, then went into his office and shut the door with the frosted glass window behind him. He hadn't stopped for more cigarettes before coming in to work this

61

morning, but he sat at the desk and pulled a spare pack from the top drawer.

Cathy's husband had emphysema, so in addition to other things, Beckett's smoking was something that Cathy gave him a hard time about on a daily basis. "Harold sucked down three packs a day for forty years," she'd say, "and now he can't go anywhere without that darn oxygen tank. You don't knock it off, that'll be you someday, mark my words."

He rolled his chair over and cracked the office window before he lit up. Part of it was because he felt guilty, but mostly he just didn't feel like hearing it today.

After he finished his smoke, he closed the window, picked up the phone, and dialed Nancy's number. He got a busy signal, so he figured he ought to call the school, confirm Missy's absence and see what other steps they'd taken, if any.

"The last day she was recorded as present," said Janine Christie, the school secretary, "was last Tuesday, the seventeenth."

"Have you contacted anyone besides the girl's mother?"

"We try to postpone contacting the authorities until we have more information. With someone like Missy, we tend to think it's trouble at home, but of course we want to be sure."

"'Someone like Missy'?" he said.

The woman on the other end of the line lowered her voice.

"Well, she's from a broken home, and frankly, the girl has a reputation, if you know what I mean."

Beckett knew, but he didn't reply.

"We plan to contact the truancy office this afternoon. It will be up to them to decide if CPS should be involved."

Beckett knew what happened to kids who got put into the system, even ones close to being adults. A lot of them ended up in far worse places than the ones they'd been taken from. He'd seen it happen too many times, especially when he worked in the city. And while Missy's home life was no doubt troubled, he suspected that particular type of intervention would only make things worse.

"If it's all the same to you, Ms. Christie, I'd like it if you held off on that until I speak with Missy's mother again. The fewer people that are called in on something like this the better—at least until we know it's absolutely necessary. From what Ms. Foster says, her girl's just home with a bug."

"Yes, that's what she says," said Ms. Christie. "But she never called to let us know. And when I told her we'd need verification of the illness soon, otherwise we'd need to report it, well, she wasn't too happy."

"No, I can't imagine she would be," he said.

"I can delay it for a day or two longer, Chief Beckett, but we're obligated to report students who miss more than five consecutive days without approved documentation. Today makes six and counting."

"Duly noted," said the chief. "I sure appreciate your cooperation on this."

He hung up the receiver and sat for a moment, then picked it back up and tried Nancy's number again. The line was still busy, and he suddenly felt himself getting restless.

Beckett left his office, and when he closed the door, Cathy sniffed the air and looked at him over the top of her thick-rimmed eyeglasses.

"What?"

"Nothing," she said. "It's your funeral."

He walked over to the coffee urn and filled his thermos for the road.

"Think I'll take a ride, make a few rounds," he said. "I'll radio in before lunch."

"I'll hold down the fort," Cathy said.

"You always do," he replied, and went back out into the cold, white morning.

#

He opted for his Bronco, deciding that the four-wheel drive would be the safer choice for his trip out to see Nancy Foster. The roads out here were already a mess, and even in the truck, the drive to Miles Junction took him twenty minutes. The little burg was unincorporated, meaning it had no governing body of its own and the policing fell to Beckett and his men. It almost always had to do with money. The town's own schools had been closed down a couple years earlier for that very reason—fiscal insolvency. The kids of Miles Junction now took buses over to Middleton like the rest of the kids in Lornfield Township. The whole thing made Beckett's job even harder. He had half a dozen officers, each working twelve-hour shifts, just to keep things going. Damn near every morning he woke up wondering if today would be the day. Pack it up. There just wasn't enough manpower. Go work security at the mall or the hospital.

Despite the hardships, however, Beckett couldn't help but appreciate the scenery as he drove. It was desolate but peaceful, like driving through a landscape that predated everything—roads, wars, economic depressions. There was no difference between the white of the land and the white of the sky above—like a single, smudged piece of parchment—and the only stark visual distinctions anywhere were those drawn by trees periodically lining the road or punctuating the distant fields in dense congregations, all bowing their heads under the enormous burden of ice and snow. Houses and battered barns peeked out from beneath heavy white hoods, and only the tops of fence posts poked through the massive drifts. Occasionally he'd see folks excavating vehicles and clearing walkways.

And the worst of it was still to come.

When he got to town, he turned right on Main Street, passed Miller's Tap and Mort's Little Shopper, and drove about a half mile farther until he reached the Foster residence. The small house was set back from the road, a rundown, sea-foam colonial with a crudely enclosed porch and fangs of frozen water hanging from its rust-eaten gutters. The stoop attached to the front was a block of concrete, on which two snow-covered lawn chairs perched flanking a boarded-up screen door. He pulled in the driveway and parked beside Nancy's mottled Ford Pinto. Behind it, a blood-red Chevy Nova that Beckett knew must belong to whoever had been in the background as they talked on the phone last night. The reason she didn't want him coming by.

He went up the steps with caution, mindful of the ice, and knocked. When no one answered, he entered and knocked on the main door. The inside porch was cluttered with moldy cardboard boxes and large garbage bags full of pop bottles and beer cans. A tattered couch sat in one corner, stuffing spewing from one of its cushions.

She opened the door, dressed in a faded pink terrycloth robe and smoking a cigarette. Her black hair was laced with threads of gray, and the creases around her eyes and mouth had grown deeper with age. She was only in her early forties, a decade younger than Beckett, but her hard living had caught up.

"Really shoulda called," she said.

"Hello, Ms. Foster," he said, glancing past her.

"Think we're way beyond that, don't you?"

He nodded slowly. "She still hasn't turned up, I take it."

"What do you think?"

"And you really got no idea where she might be?"

Nancy smirked and took a drag from her cigarette. She exhaled smoke from the corner of her mouth and said, "Shit, I can't keep track of that girl. She's been runnin' all over since God knows when."

"You don't suppose she got off to the city again, do you? After last time?"

The previous spring, Missy and a couple of her girlfriends, Rachel Schuler and Katie Price, had gone over to the truck stop on Route 7. There they met some guys who took them to a dive called The Sundown on the city's South Side. Rachel had stolen her parents' car while they were sleeping, and when she returned home late that night, they were up waiting for her. Rachel told them about everything. The three guys, the bar, how she and Katie had wanted to leave, but Missy had wanted to stay, so they left her there. Rachel's parents contacted Missy's mother, who in turn contacted Beckett. He made a call to one of his old friends with Youngstown police, but by the time they checked the Sundown, it was well past last call, and the place was locked up tight.

It was about six in the morning when a local farmer spotted Missy staggering down the center of a deserted back road on the edge of the township, looking roughed-up and dazed. Beckett was in his office at the station when the call came in, so he picked the girl up and took her home. She didn't speak a word the whole way, but she didn't need to for Beckett have an idea about what had happened. Whoever they were, they'd used her up and dumped her off in the dirt like a piece of garbage.

The memory of that night opened a pit in Beckett's stomach. That was spring, but it was now winter. And anyone out wandering for too long in this cold might not make it.

"I already called those other two skanks," Nancy said, "but they don't know nothin'. Like I'm saying, that girl's all over the place. You know that. Ain't nothin' new. I didn't think much of it till the school called."

A voice called from behind her, somewhere inside the house: "Nance, you don't got no bacon in here!"

She yelled over her shoulder: "You want bacon, you best get your ass to the store and buy some!"

When she turned to face Beckett again, he hoped she couldn't see his jaw flexing, the fire he felt flaming behind his eyes. "When was the last time you saw her?" he asked.

She thought on it for a moment. "Early last week, I guess it was."

"I can't help but notice you don't seem too concerned," he told her as she dragged her cigarette again. He wanted to snatch the thing from her lips and grind it out on the fraying door mat.

She gave him a mean look.

"If you think she's just 'shacked up with some boy,'" he said, using her own words, "but you got no idea who with or

where, then what are we"—he paused, corrected himself—
"what am *I* supposed to do? You tell me that."

Her look softened, but only a little. She said, "I can't
exactly go letting the school think I'm unfit, bring in some
home-wreckin' social worker, now can I?"

"Can't?" he asked. He thought it strange that she cared
one way or the other.

"Won't," she rephrased.

"So you want me to find her, then." It wasn't a question.

"You're a decent man, Lou, maybe one of the only ones,
when you wanna be. Anyhow, girl may be a pain in my ass,
but she's my daughter. I ain't gonna let no one take her away
just because she skips off now and then."

He didn't say anything for a moment. As much as she
riled him inside, as much as he wanted to hate her for being
the way she was, cold and crass and self-involved, she had
values deep down, twisted as they might be.

"I told you if she didn't come home, I'd see what I can
do," he said. "So I will. You have a picture of Missy I could
hold on to?"

"Nothin' recent."

"Well, you call me if she comes home, you hear?"

She nodded and closed the door.

Back in his truck, Beckett thought about the girl, how
she'd looked the night he brought her home. How there had

been something in her tired face, even at sixteen, that made him again wonder if she was his. It was no secret to him that Nancy had always been involved with other men besides him. Their own history was one of called-in favors and late-night trysts, and he knew better than to believe he was the only one. That's why things never grew beyond what they had, or what they could have had—he feared her not being faithful and feared what he might do if he found out. But not long after he'd told her he couldn't keep up the way things were between them, she was with child, allegedly by some other man. Another man that didn't stick around, so Beckett let himself get pulled in again and again whenever she found herself in rough waters. His suspicion about Missy had a lot to do with why.

Nancy never once let on that the girl might be his daughter, and Beckett never gave voice to the question that often burned in his heart because he believed he'd somehow relinquished his right to know. But still he wondered.

He pulled out onto the road and headed back toward town. As he drove, he imagined Missy out there somewhere, thought of her roaming down some potted country two-lane in the middle of the night, violated, hurt. Then he thought about the next bad storm that was slated to roll in. He imagined other things, too, horrible things, things that stoked the flames inside his chest and burned him even more as he looked out through the windshield at the cold and quiet world.

#

Morton Jeffers's daughter, Doris, who was running the store that day, told Beckett she recalled seeing Missy Foster about a week earlier when she'd been in buying vitamins and a can of lighter fluid.

"I think I remember because it was such an unusual purchase," said Doris. "Nothin' else, just those two things."

When he ducked into Miller's Tap next door, the only people in the bar—Sally the bartender and two older gentlemen, one of whom Beckett knew as Sam Harrison—hadn't seen her. In fact, they hadn't seen much of anyone, even those in the regular crowd, for a few days.

"I think a lotta folks went ahead and stocked up, bunkering down before the blizzard hits," Harrison said. "Can't say as I blame 'em, though. S'posed to get nasty."

The only other business in Miles Junction was Kurtzal's Hardware, located across the intersection from the bar. Two churches, a small grocery store with a single gas pump out front, and a tavern—besides Kurtzal's, that was it. If folks wanted to go to a restaurant, a mechanic, a Laundromat, anything, they had to go into Middleton or one of the other surrounding towns.

The job of policing an entire township with only half a dozen men, besides its logistical challenges, was hard simply because you never really got to know the people and they were so spread out. It seemed like the only citizens Beckett knew by name were the ones he'd arrested during his near twenty years on the Lornfield police force and a handful of business owners, many of whom had gone bankrupt and migrated someplace else by now. All this time and he felt like just as much a stranger to most of these people as any outsider would, especially out here, as far southeast of the county as you could get before hitting Pennsylvania.

When Beckett walked into the hardware store, the little bell that hung over the door jingled, and Walter Kurtzal turned to look from his place behind the cash register. He was Beckett's age, tall and lean with a hard-edged face and a thin gray strop of hair combed across his head. Walter was one of the few folks out here that Beckett knew personally; they'd gone to school together.

"Hey there, Walt," Beckett said.

"Hey, how you doin,' Lou?"

"Can't complain. Not that it'd do any good, anyway." They laughed. "How's business?"

"Sold some shovels yesterday. Rock salt's the hot seller right now, though. Calling for a big one tonight."

"Yeah, so I hear." Beckett removed his hat and gloves and ran a dry hand across his ash-colored crew cut. He bypassed anymore pleasantries and asked if Walt knew Missy.

"That's Nancy Foster's girl," Walt said. "Sure."

"You by chance seen her around lately?"

Walt appeared to be thinking. "No, can't say as I have. Don't see much besides the inside of the store these days, do we, Benny?"

Benny was Walt's boy, though he wasn't really a boy. The short, heavyset Benny was about thirty years old with Down syndrome, and Beckett thought he was one of the sweetest, most kind-hearted individuals he'd ever had the pleasure to meet. He was sitting on a high stool behind the counter, hard at work counting screws, removing them from one plastic container and placing them in another, and didn't respond to his father's question.

"Inventory," Walt said, winking at Beckett. "He loves to help out."

"Hey there, Benny," Beckett said, smiling when Benny looked up from his container of screws.

"Hello, Chief," he said, carefully enunciating the words and returning the smile.

Beckett walked down the length of the counter. "Givin' your old man a hand around the store, huh?"

"Yes, sir," Benny said, and his childlike smile grew even bigger.

Beckett looked around, but there was no one else in the store. The long narrow space was a maze: bins filled with nails and washers, nuts and bolts; racks of tools and spools of electrical wire; stacked bags of rock salt; shelves lined up with gumboots, flannel shirts, fishing gear, and other supplies, all in no particular arrangement.

"Girl in some sort of trouble?" Walt asked.

"Can't say," Beckett said. "But you'll call if you see her or hear anything?"

"Of course. And I'll ask anyone who comes through here, though so far it's been a slow mornin'."

"I sure appreciate that, Walt. We'll see you around, Benny."

Benny looked up from his work again.

"You take care of your old man now," Beckett said. "Don't let him work you too hard."

"Okay," he replied, and jumped up to give the chief a high five with a broad, stubby hand.

Beckett put his hat and gloves back on and returned to his truck.

What now? Short of going door-to-door, what else was there to do? He didn't have so much as a sliver of information about the girl that was useful in tracking her down.

"Door-to-door it is, then," he said to the empty cab.

For the next couple hours, Beckett did some inquiring, first at the homes closest to the center of town, then some of the outliers. Still, he turned up nothing. Folks in these small towns were known to be secretive when the law was around, at least when you needed a tip on something worth knowing about, but they were also known to look after their own. This was Missy Foster, though, daughter of Nancy Foster, whose antics preceded her at every turn, and Beckett wondered at times if people really didn't know or just didn't care.

Before heading back to the station, he radioed his two daytime officers, who were responding to separate traffic accidents, one in Middleton and one in Union, and told them to ask around before they came home. "Check every gas station, fast-food joint—anywhere else that looks like a teenage girl might go or be seen," he said. He gave them the basic information: hair, age, approximate height and weight based on his memory of her. That was all they had to go on. No photo. Not even a description of what Missy might be wearing.

Back in his office, Beckett contacted his friend with the YPD, explained the situation. He asked him to keep his eyes open and an ear to the ground.

Then he turned on the radio and listened for updates on the coming storm.

#

That night, as Beckett sat in his chair, unable to sleep, the blizzard hit, the worst northeast Ohio had seen since just after the First World War, according to later news reports. The bitter two-day storm swept into the region from the southwest, burying the entire Valley in snow. Drifts up to twenty feet in some places. Days afterward, phone lines were still down in certain areas and some folks were still without power. President Jimmy Carter declared Ohio a disaster area and ordered three hundred troops from Fort Bragg to Toledo, and The National Guard had been called in all across the state to help clear roadways, assist utility crews, and transport medical personnel to local hospitals and doctors' offices. Two people had died when a building collapsed in Youngstown, twenty-two people had been confirmed dead after being stranded outdoors in the storm, roughly a dozen had died stranded in stalled vehicles, and another dozen had frozen to death in their own homes from lack of heat.

As days passed with still no sign of Missy, Beckett feared they'd soon be adding another name to the list of unfortunate souls who lost their lives.

Each day, despite how busy they were responding to accidents and other calls, he told his men to keep looking. And each day at shift change, the news was more of the same. A lot of people knew Missy, but no one had seen her.

On Sunday evening, two days after the last flake fell, Cathy went home for the night, and Officer Franklin, a young kid, a bit clumsy but level-headed, was working dispatch. The icy roads were bound to keep his other two guys, Ritz and Deputy Chief Edwards, out most of the night, directing traffic and filling out collision reports, so Beckett stayed on at the station, rather than go home.

Sitting in his office, he smoked a cigarette but didn't bother to open the window now that Cathy wasn't there to give him any grief about it. They were going to have to form a search party. The county wouldn't spare men, and certainly not the state, not for one missing girl, not at a time like this. But maybe they could get some locals to help out.

Beckett inhaled the dry smoke, and it burned his lungs. He was stupid to think he'd be able to locate the girl himself, especially in the wake of the worst snowfall in over half a century. Yet he set out to do it on his own, with only a few officers asking around aimlessly when they had a few minutes to spare. Why? It was simple: because Nancy Foster had, in her own offhand way, asked him for help like she had so many times. And he still loved her. And he loved the girl, because although he didn't know the truth about her, he thought he might.

He heard Nancy's words: *You're a decent man, Lou, maybe one of the only ones, when you wanna be.*

Though he wasn't a praying man, he'd become one over the last few days. He prayed she was still alive, hoped her mother was right and she was just hiding out with some boy until things cleared up. Then he thought, *Maybe she doesn't want to be found.* But such an idea provoked so many fresh questions that he hardly knew where to begin.

He opened his desk drawer, lifted a stack of folders, and looked at the bottle of Wild Turkey he'd kept in there since Christmas. Beckett never wanted to be that guy: over-the-hill bachelor cop with a drinking problem. It was a damn Hollywood stereotype and he refused to step willingly into that role. He rarely drank the hard stuff, and never while on the job. But still, he'd purchased the bottle just the same. And a drink was sounding good about now, something to warm the belly and quiet the mind. Why not?

It was not yet full dark, but the futility of his search grew into an ache almost too much to bear. He cracked the window enough to flick the nub of his cigarette out into the snow and had pretty much resolved to have that drink when Franklin opened the door.

"Chief," he said, "I—" Franklin stopped himself, realizing he hadn't knocked first. He went back out and knocked.

Beckett shook his head and said, "Come on in, son."

Franklin entered again. "Sorry about that, sir."

"No harm done. What is it?"

"Sir, I just received a call about that Foster girl you've been talking about."

Beckett sat up straight in his chair.

"Caller didn't leave his name, just that he might have some information about someone by the name of Missy Foster. He sounded like a kid, said something about the old high school. But he was whispering, so it was hard to understand him. I told him to speak louder, but then he just hung up."

Beckett wished he could trace the call, maybe find out who it was, but the station's technology consisted of a few CBs, some walkie-talkies, and a couple rotary dial telephones—might as well be living in the Stone Age when it came to things like tracing calls and modern surveillance.

He kicked closed the drawer containing the bottle of bourbon.

"Good work, Franklin," he said.

"Should I radio Ritz and Deputy Edwards, sir?"

"No, the roads are still bad, and I need 'em out there," he said. "I'll handle this one myself. I'll call with my twenty if I need backup."

The chief was halfway out the door when Franklin asked, "What should I do, sir?"

"You just stay close to that phone, and keep the radio up so you don't miss me if I call." He gave Franklin a trusting nod and said, "You're in charge till I get back."

Franklin perked up and returned the gesture. "You got it, Chief," he said, but Beckett was already gone.

#

The wind howled across the flat fields and through the frozen hills, whipping brutally across Beckett's face when he got out of the truck. The school was encased, the parking lot waist high with fallen snow. It took him several minutes to trudge his way through it to the gymnasium doors which stood slightly ajar.

He knew better than to go into an abandoned building alone. Always have backup—one of the first things they teach you. But at least he'd radioed Ritz and Edwards, told them where he'd be. And Franklin, good kid. Not too bright, but competent enough when it came to the job and quick to respond.

The school was dark. Beckett's Maglite jittered off the peeling block walls and the debris-littered hallway ahead of him. He listened for movement but only heard the wind wailing through broken windows and the crunch of grit beneath his boots.

He didn't announce himself; calling out gave them a chance to run. Besides, could be anyone in the shadows. He smelled smoke in the air, probably someone burning garbage. A lot of folks did that. Trash men didn't stop everywhere out this far, and fire is cheaper than driving it to the dump.

He knew the layout of the school, had gone here himself a lifetime ago, and he tried to think of where she might be, if she was even here. And if so, why. He checked every room and office he came to. Nothing—just busted up desks and chairs. The same ones from when he was a student. Everything was the same, just older, fallen apart. *Sort of like you*, he thought. But that's what happens when there's no money and time keeps passing by. Things fall apart. It was happening everywhere

An open locker squeaked on its hinges—the wind, maybe a rat.

He came to the room with ovens lining one wall and cupboards built over a long counter, all destroyed. Home Economics, he remembered, where they taught girls to cook and be good wives. A bunch of nonsense, that was. More and more he'd come to realize that women were really the ones who got things done: raised kids, ran themselves ragged keeping things together. It was an instinct in most of them. Cathy, for instance—the station would crumble like this place if not for her.

He scanned the walls. The smell of smoke was strong here, and a thin layer of it hung like gauze in his Maglite's beam. Ahead of him there was a trashcan with flames guttering inside it, water bottles and soup cans and food wrappers all over the place. His hand instinctively went to the butt of his service revolver.

At first, he didn't see her. He had taken the bed in the corner for just a mess of rags and aprons. But then it shifted. He aimed his light at the heap on the cot. Cot? Must be from the infirmary down the hall.

"Missy?" he asked, hoping it was her and not someone else, someone violent.

You shouldn't have come alone, he thought. But it was too late now.

The figure beneath the blankets made a soft groaning sound, and an eye peeked out, its wetness caught in the light. He saw the stocking cap, the tangled red hair spilling out the sides, and moved closer. She tried to back away, but the wall stopped her.

"I need you to come with me," Beckett said, his tone gentle, concerned.

"Nuh-uh," she responded.

"Please, Missy. It's Chief Beckett, and I wanna to help you."

"I can't," she said. "They'll take him."

"What?" he said, confused. "Take who?"

Through tear-soaked sobs, she said, "My baby."

A terrible realization descended on him then.

He moved in, knowing there was nowhere for her to go, and pulled away the pile of blankets and sheets she'd buried herself in. She tugged them back for a moment, but then let go.

The smell was thick and foul. *Christ*, he thought. Her legs, the bed around her, were stained rust-brown with blood and feces and other bodily fluids. She held something in her arms, wrapped in a ratty thermal shirt.

Anything he might have said stalled in his throat as he reached toward her.

She clutched the bundle to her chest, and it let out a small whine.

He had known already, but that sound, and the way she held it to her, trying to protect it, trying to save it, confirmed that knowledge.

He unhooked his radio.

"Franklin, this is the chief," he said, and realized he was shaking by the quaver in his voice. "Get me an ambulance out here to the old school."

The officer's voice came back stitched with static. "What's goin' on, Chief?"

"Just do it," he said. "And make it quick."

The baby was still alive, but for how long he couldn't know. He covered her back up with the sheets and blankets.

"Everything's going to be all right," he told her.

The girl held her child and cried as they waited for help to arrive. And until he was alone, much later, cupping that drink between his weathered palms, he would fight the need to cry with her.

#

He wanted to go to Nancy's, drive her to St. Elizabeth's himself, but he didn't want to let the ambulance out of his sight, so he stayed close behind. The roads were tunnels of ice, walled in by plowed white mounds six feet tall, and despite the absence of traffic, the trip took them almost an hour.

Beckett called from the hospital, and though the ER was a jumble of sound, when she arrived, he heard Nancy's voice from down the hall. He stood talking with one of the doctors outside the room in which Missy lay sleeping, the beeping of a monitor sounding out her steady pulse. Nancy screamed for her daughter, and Beckett rushed to her, holding her back as she shouted and gestured wildly at the front desk staff.

The first thought that crossed his mind was that Mr. Chevy Nova was nowhere around. It didn't surprise him. He almost pointed it out, but now wasn't the time to be self-righteous, so he checked himself.

"Calm down," he told her, "or you'll only make things worse." He knew there'd be a lot of questions directed at her, suspicious doctors, social workers. They'd want to know if there was trouble at home, trouble at school. Drugs. Anything that would have led Missy to do what she had done. It wouldn't be easy for either of them, but she needed to hold herself together.

"What the hell happened?" she asked him.

He sat her down in the waiting room, in a corner where there were no people, and told her. As he spoke, he watched her face go from anger and fear to guilt and despair.

"She's going to be okay," he told her. "She was in shock, so they sedated her. She'll be out for a while. And the baby's gonna make it."

She began to cry, and he put his arm around her.

"When can I see her?"

"When she wakes up. But they'll want to keep her here for at least few days, for observation." They'd likely recommend some extended psychiatric care as well, but he didn't say as much. She had enough to process right now, to prepare herself for.

"Are they gonna take her away?" she asked, leaning into him.

He thought that they might, at least for a little while, but there was no way of knowing for sure just yet. So he said the only thing he could, that whatever happened, they'd get through it.

She looked up at him with red eyes. Tears glistened on her cheeks beneath the fluorescent lights. "Will you stay with me?" she asked. Her voice was raspy and low. After a moment, he pulled her head into his chest. He held her, but he didn't speak. He didn't need to. They'd been through so much. It was all right there between them, and they already knew the answer.

Running

I was so used to being scared and running by then, I don't know, guess I just always seen it coming. We spent a lot of years running, Ma and me. Start out seeking something better, that life we never had, just to hightail it in the night when that life went and turned its teeth on us.

There were lots of men in and out back then, men with big families and bigger plans. Something Ma thought would be good for a boy growing up. But they just took and took until, when she couldn't seem to give enough, they grew vicious. One always replaced the other. Ed was the worst of them all, though. We ran from Ed so many times, and after the first time I wondered why anyone would run from anyone more than once. But I was just a kid, and kids don't know nothing.

The last time we ran from Ed we were living in the trailer park at the bottom of the hill. That must've been five, six years back. It was sometime before Christmas, and I was in my room when I heard them starting up. There was the sound of glass breaking and heavy feet stomping past my door, and Ed was in the back bedroom destroying the place, hollering all kinds of things that didn't even sound like words. Ma opened my door and told me to hurry as we snuck down the long hallway and through the kitchen, where the few Christmas presents she'd been able to afford were torn apart and thrown all over, wrapping paper and bows ripped in jagged strips and scattered among the shards of broken dishes.

We made it out the door before Ed realized we were gone. Ma locked the doors of the old station wagon once we were inside and said, "Get down, honey," so I got down and looked up just as Ed hurled the trashcan, spreading the windshield like a spider's web. He leaped up onto the hood but took a tumble as we tore out of there.

The trailer park was shaped like a big horseshoe on a slope, and we were heading up and in instead of down and out like we should've been. I climbed out from under the dash as we neared the curve and looked back to see Ed cutting through the middle yards and coming after us.

"He's coming," I said.

"I know, sweetie," she said. "I see that rotten sonofabitch."

She jerked the wheel, plowed the wagon up the hill at the top of the shoe instead of staying on the drive and following the park around to where Ed was heading to cut us off. There were rocks and weeds scraping at our muffler and crunching beneath the wheels, and when we came out topside on Cherry Street the street lamps' light shined through the fractured windshield, painting broken black lines on everything inside the car. I watched Ma as she kept checking the mirror. Her face looked cracked in a hundred different places.

#

We went to Smitty's, who lived in a house off the main highway toward Middleton with his wife and son. Smitty was in some way related to Ed, distant cousins or something, and had more than once stepped in when Ed had been drinking and got rough. We'd never lived in a house, so it felt really big around me, like the walls were too far away and there were too many doorways and windows to keep my eyes on. I always liked coming here because it was always the same. Smitty's wife, whose name I can't for the life of me remember, maybe Sherry, gave Ma a drink of something, and the three of them sat in the kitchen talking while I went into the living room and turned on the TV.

But I didn't actually watch it. Instead I waited to make sure the grownups were distracted then crept toward door at the end of the hall, where music and the sound of clanking metal rose up from the basement. It's not that I wouldn't have been allowed down there, but it had become a sort of secret ritual for me, I guess.

Smitty's son, Kyle, he was seventeen and had always treated me like I was older, which made me feel older. He was lifting weights on a rusty bench, and for a minute I just sat in the shadows of the stairs watching him. Black Sabbath posters and pictures of girls in bikinis on Harleys and sprawled out on the hoods of muscle cars covered the cinderblock walls. There was a bed in one corner and a heavy bag hung from a stud in the ceiling. Kyle wore nothing but cutoff sweatpants and a pair of fingerless mesh weightlifting gloves as he did bench presses and drank from a gallon milk jug of water between sets. He'd just moved on to some other exercise when he spotted me.

"Shouldn't go sneaking around like that," he said. "Might just startle the wrong person. What'd I tell you about that?"

"Sorry," I said, looking at him through the gap in the railing before turning to go back upstairs.

"Now hang on a minute," he said. "Come on in and stay a while."

I came down off the steps and joined him in the middle of the room.

"My old man told me what happened to you and your Ma," he said. "That's a drag."

"Yeah," I said.

He looked at the floor for a second, as if he was really thinking hard about it. Then he looked back up at me and said, "He hit you again?"

"No, just her," I said. "But we got out before it got too bad." I tried to smile and even laugh a little, like it wasn't any big thing.

He got up from the weight bench and flipped over the cassette tape in the big stereo on his dresser. Then he went to the punching bag and laid into it a few times, fast and hard. When the music kicked on, he said, "You like Iron Maiden?"

I didn't really know, so I shrugged.

He shrugged back, then unleashed a series of punches into the bag while he danced around it. He was big and blond and stacked with muscles. I continued to watch as he pummeled the bag for the duration of a song, and when he stopped to take a break, he was breathing heavy and shiny with sweat.

The first time I'd come down here, back in summer, I'd asked Kyle where he learned how to box. He told me Smitty was a boxer in the Army and had started teaching him when he was real young.

"My dad never taught me nothing," I'd said. "Never even met him before."

He nodded toward the bag. "You wanna take a shot at it?"

"Yeah."

He laughed. "Come on, then."

I went over to the bag and he squared me up in front of it.

"Now, let's see your technique," he said.

I threw a sloppy wide hook, and it barely budged the heft of the bag. I felt embarrassed.

"It's all right," he told me. "Here, like this."

He positioned me in a stance, showed me how to shift my weight and pivot my hips. He showed me how to hold my hands, how to jab and cross and duck a blow.

"Go ahead," he said. "Try again."

There was still no power behind my effort, but it felt better, the rough of the canvass on my skin, the slight give of the bag beneath my hands.

"See, you got the hang of it now."

Ma and me had come over to stay a few times since then, and each time Kyle showed me something new. And tonight was no different.

"You been practicing what I showed you?"

"A little bit," I said.

"Well, let's see it."

I went over, got into position, and warmed up with a few rounds of my go-to combo: jab, jab, right cross, hook with the left, then an uppercut. And with this last one, I always skinned my knuckles on the bag.

"That ain't half bad," he said. "You're starting to get some force behind your punches. But you need to work on some other combinations. Don't get lazy, know what I mean?"

I nodded.

"All right, then. Let's get to work."

For the next hour or so, we took turns on the bag. We did push-ups and sit-ups and pull-ups from a pipe in the ceiling. He kept showing me things, correcting my form, and encouraging me as we boxed our way through Iron Maiden and Judas Priest.

"And remember," he told me before I went back upstairs, "it's not about how fast you are with these"—he held up his fists in front of my face— "as long as you're quicker than the other guy up here." He tapped a finger against my temple.

Upstairs, the grownups still sat in the kitchen playing cards and drinking. A pistol lay on the counter close to Smitty's right hand, and when I looked in, they all turned toward me and smiled smiles I knew were supposed to comfort me in some way but didn't.

"Don't worry, Dust," Smitty said. He was a short man, but had the look of a dog who, although gentle, could be fierce when he had to be. "Ol' Ed knows better'n to come around here." And that did comfort me, but only a little.

In the living room, I lay on the couch facing the back cushions and running my thumbs over my tender knuckles until at last, exhausted, I slept, a darkness without dreams.

#

Ma usually still had me go to school on days after our running. Guess she wanted to keep at least some kind of normal for me. But this time I went to work with her the next morning, and when the school opened, she called me in sick.

She cooked over at the Cloverleaf during breakfast. Since it was early and the bar section was closed in the morning, Ma fixed me up a bed in one of the back booths with some old aprons for a blanket, told me to try and get some more sleep, and when I couldn't sleep no more, I sat doodling and drawing pictures on paper placemats.

I didn't know when we were going home, but we always had before, eventually. After Ma got off work, we spent the rest of the day in the car eating leftover hash browns and bacon she'd taken from the restaurant and mostly stayed parked at truck stops so as not to use up gas. She used payphones to call about places to stay, but most people she knew were at work themselves when she called or else couldn't help on account of this or that. There was always Grandma's place, but Ma and her never got along too good ever since she was a girl, and the last time we went there they just spent the whole time fighting. We might have gone back to Smitty's, I suppose—I wished we would—but Ma was too prideful to ever wear out her welcome.

When we were finally out of money and couldn't even afford phone calls because she didn't get paid until the end of the week, she kept apologizing to me like she'd done something wrong, and I couldn't understand what she thought she'd done. We'd slept in the car before, so that didn't bother me none, but I could tell it bothered her a lot. Whenever she'd look over at me from the driver's seat, it was like she wanted to cry but wouldn't cry because maybe crying

94

would be the end of something, like admitting something she didn't want to admit.

"I never meant for any of this," she'd say. "You know that, right, Dustin?"

"Yeah, Ma, I know," I'd say as we huddled together in front of the heating vents to keep warm until we eventually had to shut off the engine.

That night, it got so cold I woke up and couldn't feel my toes and my body was clenched tight from shivering and all my muscles were sore. Ma was gone, and for a moment I thought she'd left me, but then I saw her out there and knew I never should've thought such a thing. We were at a friend of hers place, a man named Steve, who lived in a big blue house beside the Dairy Queen and took us in sometimes.

She was creeping around in the bushes by the house, tossing small rocks and whisper-shouting at an upstairs window. It was one of the first times I saw just how desperate we were. We had nothing and no one but each other, and I think Ma was finally realizing maybe that wasn't enough. I imagined Ed's face, twisted, on those nights when I knew something bad was on its way to happening, when furniture and things would get knocked around and busted and maybe even Ma if things got real bad. And as I thought about it all, the red light from the Dairy Queen sign poured across the hood of the station wagon and all I could think was that it looked like blood.

#

Steve finally woke up and let us in after a bit and set me up in the spare room, which he'd turned into a small movie theater. He was tall and skinny with dark hair and big old eyeglasses that made him look like a cartoon and was into computers and inventing stuff. His house was full of electronics and homemade gadgets. He was a nice guy. But whenever I caught myself thinking this, I remembered they were all nice guys until they weren't.

I stayed awake all that night watching movies on a screen that took up an entire bedroom wall, playing tapes from Steve's collection which filled rows of shelves beside the bed. I watched Arnold Schwarzenegger and Sylvester Stallone take out bad guys, and I felt my blood moving faster at the sight of it. The violence and broken bones. The red.

Sometime in the early morning, before the sun came up, I went to the bathroom and heard Ma and Steve talking behind a closed bedroom door. Their voices were muffled, and there were long spots of silence each time one of them said something. All I could make out was her saying she was sorry—she was always apologizing about something—and Steve saying he was sorry, too, but he couldn't keep doing this and this morning we would have to leave and for us to please not come back.

I returned to the spare room, put on another movie, and lay there, wondering what we would do, where we would go if we couldn't go home.

After a while, I grew restless and wished I was still back in the basement with Kyle. So while Rocky Balboa trained on a mountain in the snow, heaving rocks and hauling logs, I did push-ups and sit-ups until my body no longer ached, until I couldn't feel anything at all. And when the time came for him to fight the big Russian twice his size, I stood on the bed and threw punches. I danced in circles in front of the screen and thought about all those times running. I jabbed and ducked and shifted my body until I thought my heart would explode.

Eventually, I collapsed on the mattress, my lungs on fire. But as I lay gasping, I saw faces floating in front of my eyes—saw the Eds and Bobs and Kennys and Jakes—and when the faces grew their numbers, I reminded myself that Ma and me, we were all we had in this world. And that's when I pulled myself back up, still out of breath, and started swinging.

Letting Go

for Dolores

Bobby Voss sat at the end of the bar, the corner closest to the jukebox, and as the last few people who'd attended Dee's funeral straggled in, he was already working on his second shot and chaser. He hadn't stayed until the end of the service, couldn't stand it anymore—everyone bowing their heads and wiping their noses, looking so damn sober and sad. The last thing Dee would have wanted was for people to mull about mourning her. "Get your heads outta your asses," she would've said. "Stop puttin' up such a fuss." But what really got to Bobby was the fact that no one gave two shits one way or another that Dee was gone, except that it meant one less person to get generous and buy rounds on the first of the month. And now they'd brought their insincere grief back to the bar with them, putting their arms around one another, raising their glasses, and getting nostalgic.

After his third drink, Bobby went to the juke, popped in a quarter, and punched some random numbers, not really caring what came on so long as it drowned out the noise a little. Back on his stool, he waited for Sally, the bartender, to bring him another beer while he munched stale pretzels and stared at the Polaroid photograph in his other hand.

Meanwhile, people kept on drinking, talking, and telling lies.

Sam Harrison was at the opposite corner of the bar, his usual spot, looking stoic and wise with his silver hair and two-tone beard. *He's good people*, Bobby thought, the only one in the lot of them other than Sally and maybe Joan Simpkins, an older gal who had played Bridge with Dee a couple nights a week. The rest of the crowd, however—good enough to drink with, he supposed.

A pall of tobacco smoke stretched across the bar in an ever widening, ever thickening canvas. Through the haze, he watched and listened to Wade Little, who wasn't little at all but about six and a half feet tall and built like freight car. He was standing next to Gil Cunningham and Roger Kneff on the other side of the room, his loud voice carrying over the music.

Wade began telling a story about how he'd done some snow removal and other odd jobs for Dee over the years.

"Time's been tough since seventy-seven, seventy-eight," Wade said. "First the mills, then the blizzard. Ol' Dee helped me out, though. Kept the power on, at least."

The others nodded, as if each had a similar memory of Dee's charitable nature.

With each new anecdote, someone would raise a glass and say, "To Dee," and the others would follow suit, toasting the woman they all claimed to adore.

Maybe it was the bottom-shelf whiskey that did it, but after about ten minutes of listening to Wade and his

100

companions go on jawing, Bobby couldn't keep his mouth shut any longer.

"Seventy-eight was bad all right," he said, raising his voice so they all knew he had joined the conversation. "Lot of folks needed work. Lot of folks paid for services never rendered, too, if I'm not mistaken."

They all looked at Bobby, who had put the Polaroid back in his breast pocket and was now clicking the lid of his Zippo while he spoke.

"In fact, if my memory serves, Dee gave you an advance, didn't she, Wade? Exclusive dibs on snow in the winter, grass in the summer, and leaves in the fall. So tell us, how many times did you get over that way, you know, to do the job you were paid to do?"

Wade Little's flat pug face sagged, as if suddenly losing its battle against gravity.

"What are you gettin' at, Voss?" he asked.

"Oh, just that maybe things aren't always the way we remember 'em."

The process of reading between the lines seemed to cause Wade physical discomfort, and he finally said, "You callin' me a liar?"

"If the shoe fits," Bobby said, punctuating the end of the statement with the Zippo: Clink.

"You oughta slow down, bud, 'fore you get yourself all worked up," Wade said.

"First of all, I ain't your bud, Wade"—Clack— "so let's go ahead and clear that up right now. Second,"—Clink— "you left Dee snowed in for nearly five days one time before she finally called someone else to come over." Clack. Bobby stared at him, challenging Wade to respond.

"For your information," Wade said, intoning as much self-righteousness as his pea-sized brain could muster, "my truck was broke down for a while, not that it's any business of yours. A lot of us were snowed in that year."

"I don't suppose you ever paid her back for the days you failed to show up, though?" Clink. Bobby didn't give him a chance to say anything else. "No, of course not. Spent it all by then, right?" Clack.

Bobby was on his feet by then, walking down to their end of the bar. So far, no one else had bothered to chime in.

But the others weren't off the hook.

He was tired of Wade already, so Bobby turned his eyes on Gil Cunningham. "And what about you?" he said.

Gil sat up, looking confused. "Wuddaya mean, me?"

"You want me to get started on that half-assed duct tape job you passed off as plumbing when Dee paid you to fix her burst pipes? 'Cause I'd be happy to talk about that, if you want."

Gil just stared down at the bar, didn't even comment.

Roger was next.

Bobby directed his gaze at the man. "And how much did you still owe her on that Riviera, the one she let you make payments on, the one she signed over to you up front and let you have in good faith? What was the story you gave her, the reason you didn't have the money month after month? What was it? Child support payment? Or maybe it was fines from that DWI you got when you totaled your last car. Whatever it was, I'm sure you were real convincing."

"It's not like she drove the damn thing, anyway," Roger said. "She told me I could pay when I was able."

Bobby laughed. "It's funny that no matter how strapped everyone is, they manage to drink away hours a day in this goddamn place." He shook his head, and finished the rest of his beer.

"Who the hell do you think you are, Bobby?" Roger said, going from embarrassed to indignant. "You think you're some kind of saint or something?"

"Me?" Bobby said. "Nah, I'm far from it. But then, I don't pretend to be, neither."

They'd all been looking at him, but now turned their eyes away.

Wade motioned for Sally to bring him a refill.

"Each one of you acts like you went out of your way to do things for Dee," Bobby said, "when it was only ever you dipping your hand in her pockets because she was good enough to let you take advantage. And I'll guarantee she never once called any of you out on it, because that wasn't her style."

Bobby had Sally pour him another shot and beer. When she placed them in front of him, he emptied the draft in three gulps, but held off on the shooter.

No one had really engaged in Bobby's deliberate confrontation, most likely because they all knew he spoke the truth. The rest of the patrons—some regulars, some friends of the regulars—sat talking amongst themselves, drinking their drinks and not paying the scene much mind.

Bobby lit a cigarette, pocketed the Zippo, and reiterated: "Nope, I'm no saint. Hell, I might be just as much of a piece of shit as the rest of you for all I know." He took a pull from the cigarette and exhaled two streams of smoke through his nose. "Now, Dee," he continued. "That old broad was a damn saint."

Bobby stood for a long minute just staring at the wall across the bar. Dee had often told him that every moment of every day we stand at a fork in the road, that while God knows our choices before we do, he still gives us the will to decide. Bobby didn't know about all that, but he did know that he stood at such a place now.

"To Dee," he finally said, raising the shot glass. There was hesitation, but several others soon joined him in the toast. He downed the shot, and as it burned its way through him, Bobby held the glass in his fist, feeling its weight.

The conversation began to pick back up. He snubbed his cigarette out in the metal ashtray on the bar and tightened his fist around the small glass.

Finally, Bobby said, "As for the rest of you . . . well, you can just go fuck yourselves." Then he hurled the shot glass. Wade, despite his size, moved out of the way as it sailed past his face, close enough that he must have felt the breeze. The glass shattered against the wall above the pinball machine.

A murmur of surprised voices erupted, the scraping sound of stools being pushed away from the bar. Wade had Bobby by the collar before the pieces of glass had finished settling on the floor. "You got a real problem, you know that?" Wade said to him through clenched teeth.

"Maybe you're not as dumb as you look, Wade," Bobby said.

Wade gut-punched him.

"Jesus Christ!" Sally shouted. "Take it outside!"

Wade began dragging him toward the door, but Sam Harrison and someone Bobby didn't know intervened.

"You little cocksucker!" Wade yelled from behind a wall of men. "I'm gonna whup your ass, boy!"

"Get outta here, Bobby," Sam said, escorting him out the door into the overcast April afternoon. "Get some air, and get your head together, for Christ's sake."

"Suppose I could stand to anyway," Bobby said. "The bullshit in there's thick enough to choke us all."

"You really are a crazy sonofabitch, Bobby, you know that?"

"Hey, don't go gettin' my mom involved, now," Bobby said. "That's disrespectful." Then Bobby grinned and put up his dukes, danced around Sam Harrison like a fighting leprechaun in the gravel parking lot.

They both laughed. Bobby stopped and patted the older man on the shoulder, a gesture that seemed to express a repressed gratitude.

When Bobby climbed into his beat-up Bonneville and started the engine, Sam said, "You really think you should be drivin'?"

Bobby shut the door, looked at the man through the open window as he put the car in gear. "You know something, Sam?" he said. "You're all right."

#

Bobby drove to the outskirts of town, meandered along winding two-lanes banked with scrub and maple and the last lingering patches of a late March snow. When he again neared town, he turned onto Hillstead, passing ramshackle houses with stripped siding, clothes lines sagging above dead lawns, and broken-down campers in rutted driveways. About a mile up, where the street curved and sloped down to Main, he slowed to a stop.

To the right was St. John's, where he'd accompanied Dee a few times for worship, despite his reservations. It meant a lot to her, he knew that, so he kept his doubts to

106

himself. Above the arched doorway was a single word inscribed in the wide keystone: Sanctuary. A place of refuge. It was something everyone sought at one time or another, and for Bobby Voss, the first time had come when he was only eleven years old.

It was the summer of 1968, the weekend he and his mother had first moved to Miles Junction. His father had laid down his chopper on an icy switchback and slid right into the path of a box truck when Bobby was only three years old, so now it was just the two of them. Well, mostly. They'd rented an old garage apartment at the bottom of a long, eastward sloping drive that intersected the main road into Pennsylvania and disappeared into an overgrown field that stretched all the way to the turnpike. That night, the yard was full of motorcycles and rusted-out cars, while the small residence was full of pale women with husky voices and scary-looking men with names like Chewy, Red Dog, and Spider. His mother's friends. She'd always had friends like these. They'd be in and out for a while, eventually replaced by a new cast of characters, just like the others—bloodshot eyes and smelling like gasoline.

Around eleven o'clock that night, Bobby found himself sitting on the cement steps while the party geared up inside. He'd been in his bedroom, lying on the mattress on the floor and listening to the sounds of the adults in the main room (sounds he struggled to interpret because even the laughter sounded like fighting) when a bearded man in a leather vest and a skinny, black-haired woman with lots of silver bracelets and a gap between her front teeth came in. They started kissing and taking off their clothes right in front of him, as if he wasn't even there.

He snuck outside and tried to read a well-thumbed Spiderman comic under the sallow porch light but couldn't concentrate on anything but the pictures. After several minutes of flipping through the pages, he put the comic down beside him and began chucking pebbles at a beer bottle that sat crooked in a clump of grass beside a Harley's front tire. The late-summer air was warm against his skin. The sky was ribbed with thin clouds and illuminated by a sliver of moon that looked like a clipped fingernail.

The voices and music inside rose and fell and blended together until they were eventually just a singular, warbled chorus of sound with no words.

He was tired and wanted to be in his bed, but his bed had been taken and he was just a lousy kid who couldn't do anything about it.

Then, as he contemplated curling up on the step and trying to sleep, a gravelly voice came out of the darkness: "Little late to be outside at your age, isn't it?"

Bobby looked up and saw a woman standing in the side doorway of the only other house on the drive, which sat a couple hundred yards away. She was silhouetted against the light behind her and close enough that she didn't have to talk much above normal. He didn't respond to her question and continued to throw rocks at the discarded bottle, bigger ones now, until finally it broke.

"Looks like a real shindig goin' on down there," she said.

This time he replied, "Yeah, I guess."

She reached her arm inside the door and flipped a switch, bringing to life a glass covered light fixture on the porch. He could tell that she was old because of her short, curly white hair and big-framed eyeglasses, but her features were still mostly in shadow.

"What's troublin' ya, kid?" she asked. "You got a look on your face like someone your age ought not have."

He shrugged, not getting her meaning.

There was a minute of silence then, and, as if losing her patience, the old woman said, "Well, all right," and turned to go back inside. But she stopped and looked back at him. "Anyhow," she said, "door's open if you need to use it."

When she was gone, Bobby sat for a while, staring blankly at the woman's house. It was a small single-story home, surrounded by blackberry brambles which had begun to obscure some of the windows. The roof sat at a steep angle, and the siding was the color of bleached bone. Lit only by its own porch light and the moon's faint radiance, Bobby thought the place looked like something out of a fairytale.

His mother and her friends continued drinking and smoking and being loud inside. At one point, a shirtless man with tattoos covering his arms stumbled out onto the porch and began urinating in the bushes a few feet away from Bobby, muttering to himself and blind to the boy's presence.

When he finished, he zipped up his jeans and noticed Bobby sitting there. "Hey, man," the guy said in a sloppy voice from behind a cigarette, "you got any pills?"

Bobby looked at the man and said, "I'm only eleven."

The man looked confused for a moment, as if suddenly unsure where he was, and then started muttering again as he disappeared back inside.

Bobby once more turned his eyes toward the old lady's house. He could see her outline through the window, moving back and forth in what he guessed was the kitchen. Then, almost without thinking, he stood up, tucked the comic book into the back pocket of his jean shorts, and walked up the drive.

He tapped lightly and then reluctantly opened the door. As he crossed the threshold, the smell of cooked cabbage and potatoes, both of which filled large bowls on a long table, greeted him. He stood there in the kitchen, alone, feeling like he was somewhere he didn't belong. A moment later, just as Bobby was about to turn around and leave, the old woman appeared, a bag of flour in her hand and a dish towel draped over her shoulder. She was dressed in fuzzy slippers, sweatpants, and faded T-shirt bearing the Pittsburgh Steelers logo.

"Decided to come visit after all, huh?" she said.

Bobby didn't move at first, just looked around the room as she continued puttering around the kitchen. Beside the mixing bowls filled with cabbage and potatoes was a mound of dough. After sprinkling flour out on the table, she picked up the dough and slammed it down, sending up a light puff of dust, then began flattening it out with a rolling pin.

Finally, she said, "You gonna just stand there not sayin' anything? 'Cause if you are, you mind helpin' out a little?"

"Sure," Bobby said. "What should I do?"

"For starters, you got a name?"

"Bobby," he said, "Bobby Voss."

"Well all right, Bobby Voss, take that there drinking glass on the counter and hand it to me, would ya?"

Bobby did as she asked.

"Now what I want you to do is flip the glass over and press the rim of it into the dough like this." She demonstrated for him, cutting a perfect circle into the flattened dough. Then she let him try.

He took the glass from her and did exactly what she had done. "Like that?" he asked.

"Already a professional," she said.

Bobby took it as a compliment and smiled. "What's all this for?" he asked.

"Pierogies," she said. The word sounded strange as it rolled off her tongue, like some other language.

"Pier what?"

"Pierogis," she said, and laughed. "They're Polish, sorta like a little dumpling you can fill with all kinds of stuff. You know what a dumpling is?"

He didn't but said, "I think so."

She walked to the freezer, got some ice, and added several cubes to a different glass that sat on the counter.

"Are they good?"

"Of course they're good," she said, pouring some type of liquor into the glass and topping it off with some ginger ale that she got from the refrigerator. "Tell me, you think I'd be makin' 'em if they weren't?"

"No, I guess not," he said, feeling a little foolish.

"I'm Dolores," she told him. "But my friends call me Dee, so I suppose you can call me that, too."

"Okay," he said.

"You want some ginger ale? Or I think I have some cocoa in the pantry if you'd like that instead."

"No, thank you."

Bobby finished cutting the dough, and then he helped Dee spoon small amounts of the filling into the centers of the circles, after which they folded them to form small pockets, and sealed the edges by pressing down on them with a fork. While they worked, she asked him why he'd been sitting outside by himself so late at night, but rather than recount the story, he simply said that he liked it there. A look crossed Dee's face that seemed partly amused and partly sympathetic, but before she could press him on the subject, Bobby asked, "How come you're making"—he hesitated on the word— "pierogis so late at night?"

"Oh, I'm a bit of night owl," she said.

"But I thought old people went to bed early."

She eyed him like she was offended and then broke out laughing. "Why you little son of a gun."

She seemed to get a real kick out of it, so he asked, "How old are you, anyway?"

She continued to laugh and said, "Didn't anyone ever tell you it's not polite to ask a woman her age?"

He had in fact heard that before, but didn't admit to it.

"But if you must know, I'm sixty-one if I'm a day."

"I turned eleven last winter," Bobby said, figuring she would probably ask, though once he offered up the information she didn't reply. She pulled a long, skinny cigarette from a brown leather case on the counter and lit it with a lighter that her knobby thumb struggled to strike.

Then Bobby heard someone calling his name. It was his mother. She must have finally noticed he was gone.

"I should go," he said.

"Well, thanks for your help, Bobby. Tell you what, drop by tomorrow afternoon. These'll be all ready for eatin' by then."

"Okay, thanks."

She smiled at him in a grandmotherly way and said, "You're all right, kid."

He smiled back and started out the door.

"Wait a second, Bobby." She reached into a small tin that sat on a shelf above the stove and removed a five-dollar bill. "Here, this is for you."

"What's this for?" he asked.

"For making my job a little easier. I see you got one of them comic books in your back pocket. Maybe go and buy yourself some new ones if you want. Heck, do whatever you like with it. It's yours. You earned it."

He tucked the money in the pocket of his shorts and thanked her again before walking back down the drive toward home. By the time he got there, his mom had returned to the party. She had already forgotten he wasn't there.

#

Bobby's drive had brought him nearly full circle. And now he sat parked in front of the small garage apartment where he'd lived with his mother. It was still boarded up, the bricks around the windows and doors still stained black from the blaze that devoured everything inside. One of his mother's boyfriends had been playing chemist in the kitchen, and the landlord never bothered to renovate.

Up the slope, a car sat parked in front of Dee's place. Mercedes. Washed and waxed. It took him a moment to realize why the vehicle struck him as familiar, but as he walked toward it and caught his reflection in its tinted glass, he remembered. Earlier, at the funeral, it had been parked alongside the grass between two pockmarked pickups, as out of place as a nun in a poker game.

The side door of the house was open, so he got out of his car and went inside. The gloom overtook him, but his eyes adjusted quickly. Dust-infused light seeped through random cracks in the plastic window blinds, lending a sickly hue to the place. The stillness was that of a tomb, the air dry and stale.

Somewhere in the house, the sound of a drawer being closed, another one being opened, disrupted the silence.

Bobby moved through the kitchen, into the living room, and down the short hall, where a shapeless shadow moved on the hallway wall opposite Dee's bedroom door.

He approached quietly and peered in. A late-middle-aged woman sat on the edge of the bed, the contents of a drawer—clothing, papers, what looked like a small lock box—strewn on the mattress beside her.

"Who the hell are you?" he asked.

The woman jumped, placed a hand to her chest. Her surprise lasted only a moment, however. Now she glared at him. "I'm Janice," she said, the authoritative tone in her voice suggesting some sort of dominant position in life. She stood up. "Who the hell are you? And what the hell are you doing in my mother's house?"

"Mother?" Bobby said. "Dee's your mother?"

"Was," she said.

He leaned against the dresser.

She was a well put together fifty-something, though the sense of strain in her expression gave her the look of someone ten years older. She didn't resemble Dee at all, with the exception of her eyes, which possessed a kind dignity that belied her anger. Being Dee's daughter, she hadn't come from money, though between the Mercedes and the way she was dressed, it appeared that she had found her way into it somehow. She wore high-end attire: black skirt, gray blouse, and shoes that Bobby suspected cost more than all the clothes he owned combined. Gold jewelry, modest yet clearly quite valuable, complimented her long neck and angular face, her boney wrists, and her thin fingers. Even the silver that laced her styled hair looked expensive.

She put down a stack of pictures and repeated: "Tell me who you are and what you want, or I'm calling the police." She moved around the bed, keeping her eyes on him, and picked up the phone on the nightstand. "Now," she said.

"It's Bobby Voss," he said, raising his hand for her to hold off as she dialed the 9. "Dee was a good friend of mine. I just saw the car and the open door and wanted to know who was in here."

She seemed to relax a little, and after a moment put the phone back in its cradle.

"You were friends?" she asked. "Kind of young. What are you, thirty?"

"Thirty-four, actually," he said. "I knew her since I was a kid."

"Well, that's real nice, but now isn't a good time," she said, shoving past him.

He remained in the tiny room for a moment. Almost everything in here had been packed away in boxes; about eight of them sat stacked on the far side of the bed.

When he returned to the kitchen, she was checking her face in a small compact mirror. After plucking something from the corner of her eye, she snapped it closed and placed it back into a sleek handbag which lay on the table.

He lingered in the doorway.

Finally, she said, "The last time I spoke to her was two years ago, over the phone. I didn't even know she was sick."

"I don't think anyone knew," Bobby said. "She never showed it."

Except that wasn't entirely true. He had seen the prescription bottles in the bathroom. Blood thinners, heart meds, things with names he couldn't pronounce. But she never seemed ill, so he never asked. He figured it was her business, and that she'd bring it up if she wanted to.

He hadn't been by for a while, at least a month. He'd been working a construction job out of town, clearing a lot for a new shopping mall down in Cincinnati after the first thaw in early March. Nothing permanent, but you've got to go where the money is. Now, though, as he thought about Dee and whatever secret ailments she might have had—there was no telling what she'd been like in the very end.

"They said her heart just stopped beating. I got the call two days after they found her," Janice said. "Asked if I would be able to make the service arrangements." She slid one of the chairs out from the table, its old wood creaking as she sat down and looked past him. "And then there's the rest of it."

Bobby looked over his shoulder at more boxes stacked in the corner of the living room.

"Looks like you've gotten a bit done already," he said.

"I haven't been able to do a damn thing," she replied. "It was like this when I got here."

Bobby hadn't gotten farther than the kitchen that day, hadn't seen the boxes, and it occurred to him now that Dee had begun packing herself because she'd seen it coming.

As if reading his mind, Janice said, "She must have known she didn't have long."

Despite his thinking the same thing, Bobby didn't know what to say.

"The last time we spoke, she asked me to visit," said Janice. "She always asked, and I always told her I couldn't get away. Too busy. And now . . ."

She trailed off but didn't have to finish the sentence for Bobby to know what she was feeling; he was no stranger to regret.

Several loud seconds ticked by on a wall clock, and he asked, "What's gonna happen to everything?"

"Pack the rest of it up, ship it back to Connecticut," she said. "Put it in storage until I have more time to go through it all."

"How long are you here?"

"I'm due back in Hartford in a few days. Should be enough time to box up what's left of it."

The thought of Dee's stuff sitting in some storage locker, moth-eaten and forgotten, made Bobby feel emptier than he'd felt in years, probably since his mother skipped town while out on bond for a long list of drug charges. She'd never even told him goodbye. He still found himself waiting sometimes, hoping, for a phone call or a postcard—anything at all that let him know she remembered she still had a son.

"I could give you a hand if you want," he told Janice. "It's no bother."

As if not hearing him, she said, "I could really use a drink."

Bobby walked over to the cupboard above the sink where Dee kept her bottle of Brookside. It was a little over half full. He picked up two water-spotted glasses from the dishrack and went to the table, sat down, and poured two fingers into each.

She drank, made a face, and said, "Christ, this is terrible. I never could stand this crap."

"Here," Bobby said, walking to the fridge and removing a near empty two liter of ginger ale and a tray of ice from the freezer above. He dropped three cubes into her glass and topped it off with the ginger ale. "Maybe this will help."

#

He was surprised by how naturally they seemed to get along. Her initial crassness and anger, justified as it was, fell away little by little until it was as if they were old friends.

They moved about the kitchen, Janice wrapping dishes in old newspaper and placing them in the boxes which Bobby had assembled from a flat stack in the basement. Over the course of several hours, they packed and talked. He glossed over his tumultuous childhood, about his own mother and the crowd she ran around with, but Bobby told Janice about the first time he met her mother and how she was one of the first and last friends he'd ever had. He learned that Janice had hit the ground at a sprint straight out of high school, married into Real Estate, divorced ten years later, and built her own successful agency, all without ever looking back.

"The Podunk life wasn't for me," she said, then added, "no offense."

"None taken," he replied. "If only we all had your gumption. This would be a goddamn ghost town."

Once in a while, they took a break to have another Brookside and ginger ale.

Now on their fourth or fifth drink (Bobby had only vaguely been keeping track) they sat in the living room, each in a tattered, floral patterned armchair facing the dusty television set and empty fireplace. Between them was a round table with a built-in lamp and magazine rack, its wood scuffed and worn. Dee's tan leather cigarette case was still there next to the glass ashtray. Her bible with the gilded edges was there, too. The dish still filled with sticky butterscotch candy and those airy, pastel butter mints that look like Easter. All was as it had been—at least when it came to these details.

He offered one of the cigarettes to Janice, but she declined. He removed one for himself, lit it. It was harsh and stale, so he snubbed it out after only a few drags.

"My God," Janice said, getting up from her chair and approaching the mantle. She examined the graduation picture that was on display with a variety of other knick-knacks and Pittsburgh Steelers memorabilia. "I can't believe I ever looked that young." She shook her head in disbelief. "I left that very same weekend," she said.

Though she wasn't looking at him, Bobby nodded. "Lotta folks talk about it," he said, thinking about all the times he'd made his own grand plans to do so, how often he still did, usually in those transient moments at the bottom of the bottle when anything seemed possible. "You might be the first person I ever met who actually did it, though."

"I should have come back sooner," she said, personal reproach mingling with watered down liquor.

Bobby tried to imagine what she must be feeling. Earlier he'd thought, when sensing her remorse, that guilt was a universal thing, but now he wasn't so sure. He was beginning to think that his and hers were unique, and that hers had been simmering for a long while.

"She forgives you," he told her. "I'd put money on that."

And he would. He was certain that Dee was incapable of resentment, which is why she didn't let the actions of people like Wade Little and the rest of them make her bitter. So why then was he having so much trouble convincing himself that she would have forgiven him, too, for not being here in the end?

"Maybe so," said Janice, "but that doesn't make it any easier."

This was the second time this afternoon that Bobby felt as though they were sharing some mental connection. Before he had a chance to think about how it might change the weight of the conversation, he said, "I'm the one who found her." It was the first time he'd said it out loud to anyone besides the police and the paramedics.

Janice turned from the picture she'd been staring at and returned to the chair.

"What?"

"Right there," he said, pointing toward the kitchen. "On the floor. She looked like she was just taking a nap. Couldn't have been there long."

He chose to spare her the whole truth: that Dee had been there at least long enough for her creased complexion to turn waxy and gray, that the sour smell had begun to gather about her like a cloud.

"I suppose she looked sorta peaceful," he said.

They both sat and let their eyes wander around the room, eventually settling on the spot of linoleum where he'd found Dee's body. They didn't talk for several minutes, finishing their drinks in silence.

After a while, Bobby got up and paced back and forth a few times in front of the window before stopping to gaze past the chokecherry thicket growing along the edge of the yard. The neighbor's lawn beyond was uncut and planted with junked cars, tractor motors, and heaps of old tires. The sun was starting to fade, and in the dying light the scene resembled a graveyard.

He turned back toward Janice. "Ready for another?"

She considered, then said, "Sure."

She followed Bobby back into the kitchen and began poking through cupboards that still contained a few things while he fixed the drinks.

"What's this?" she asked. She held out a small tin with a piece of paper taped to the side. "Has your name on it."

Bobby took it and opened the lid. In the tin was a roll of bills, hundreds and twenties mostly, some tens and fives mixed in.

His eyes widened for a moment, then narrowed as his forehead furrowed in confusion.

He looked up at her, his thumb running across the edges of the rolled bills. "There must be a few grand here," he said, tilting it toward her so she could see. "What's this all about?"

Janice cocked a manicured eyebrow and shrugged. "She must have meant for you to have it, I guess," she said. "Is there anything else in it?"

Rolled into the center of the bills was a small folded piece of paper. He removed it and read the short note, written in Dee's unsteady hand:

Bobby,

I've been putting a little aside for a while now, because I knew this day was bound to come sooner or later. And, let me tell you, I'm glad it was later. You take this and do whatever you want with it—it's yours. Maybe take a trip, live a little. Or if there's something you need, well, I hope it helps some.

Goodbyes are hard, so I won't drag this out any longer than need be. I'm blessed to have known you, Bobby. You made an old broad not mind sticking around so long, even when she should have called it quits years ago. I love ya, kid. Remember that. See you in the clouds.

Your Friend,

-Dee

Bobby read the letter at least three times through, then folded it and tucked it into his breast pocket behind the Polaroid photo he kept there.

After some time standing silent, at a loss for what to do, Bobby looked up when Janice said, "I hate to cut this short, Bobby. It's been nice talking with you, and I really appreciate you giving me a hand around here. It's helped make things less overwhelming today. But my head's aching and I think I ought to lie down for a little while before going back to my hotel."

Bobby wrestled with the heavy thoughts that filled his head. Looking at Janice, it was clear she indeed needed some sleep, something to eat. Her eyes were rheumy, her face pallid and expressionless.

"Yeah," Bobby said, "no problem." He held the money out to her, his eyes moving from the loose coil of bills back to her. "Here, to help with the moving truck and storage."

"No," she said, waving it away. "Keep it. She wanted you to. I'll take care of all that."

Bobby put the money in the pocket of his jeans, only half aware he had done so.

Janice went to her purse and came back with a business card with her number on it. She jotted something on the back, another number. "Keep in touch," she said. "There's my home phone. And if you want to stop by Monday morning before I leave, I'll be here early."

"Sure," Bobby said. "I will."

Back in his car, he reached for a cigarette and realized he had pocketed Dee's leather case. His eyes got bleary as he flipped open his Zippo and lit one. It was harsh and stale. But this time he smoked the whole thing.

#

Back in the center of town, Bobby went into Mort's Little Shopper for a bag of potato chips and a can of Coke. Standing under the overhang outside, a sterile fluorescent light humming above him, he ate the chips, their greasiness coating his mouth and lining his stomach. The cola was cold and bubbly; it burned his mouth and made his head tingle. When he'd emptied it, he deposited the can and crumpled bag into the trashcan by the fuel pump. Then, leaving the Bonneville parked between two faded yellow lines on the pitted asphalt, he crossed the lot toward Miller's Tap.

Since leaving Dee's, his thoughts had been so many and so fast, it was as if he weren't really thinking at all. Perhaps

126

that's why, when Bobby found himself standing at the rail waiting for Barb, the night bartender, to make her way down to his end, he felt a sense of dislocation. Like he had just arrived here, not quite sure how.

The place had filled up by now. The music was loud, the smoke thick.

"You ain't planning anything stupid, are you, Bobby?" Barb asked when she saw him waiting.

His autopilot switched back over to manual. "Now when have I ever?" he said, smiling.

"I heard about earlier," she told him. "We're not gonna have any more of that?"

Bobby didn't say yes, but he didn't say no. Instead, he said, "How about something to wet the whistle?"

"The usual?"

He nodded, and as she ventured down the bar toward the beer taps, he thumbed the lid of his Zippo and looked at the Polaroid he'd been carrying since before the funeral. The memory resolved in Bobby's mind, vivid enough to be playing out right in front of him.

It's the night of his thirtieth birthday, the night Dee gave him a new Polaroid camera as a gift. They're sitting down on the other end of the bar, but the place is packed with regulars. Dee's buying drinks for everyone and sucking down 7&7s because the bar doesn't carry the forty-two proof stuff she usually drinks at home. She always puts them away just as quickly, however, and it's not long before she's lit up like a Christmas tree.

Earlier, Bobby's mother ran off with the little bit of savings he'd put aside. An entire summer of hauling scrap and scrubbing dishes at the Idle Hour Diner. She's on another run with one of her boyfriends, and he knows it might be a week or more before she returns, looking used up and broken down. She's been doing it his whole life.

"You gotta learn to let things go, Bobby," Dee tells him as he sits gritting his teeth and cursing the woman who brought him into the world. "Let me tell you something. People aren't gonna change until they're ready to change. And your mom needs to get to that place on her own. There's nothing you can do 'cept love her as best you can. No sense gettin' hung up on what she's doin' out there. It's bad for the digestion."

"Don't know if I can," he says. "It's hard."

"Of course you can. She's your mother. And of course it's hard. Life's hard. Now quit your gripin' and take my picture, would ya'?"

As was her way, Dee had pulled Bobby from the muck of his own mind that night with a simple imperative and a dose of tough love. Just like that. And he had felt better. He tested out his new gift, snapping a photo of Dee. A big smile split her flushed face in two just below her thick bifocals. Not fifteen minutes later, she removed her brassiere through the sleeve of her blouse and flung it onto the ceiling fan. The bar rioted with laughter and raised glasses. The undergarment twirled there through the smog of cigarette and cigar smoke for nearly a week before someone finally took it down.

Bobby smiled at the memory, and when Barb returned with his shot and beer, he downed them quickly.

A worried look played at the edge of Barb's features. "Another?" she said with a note of hesitation.

Bobby said, "You know, I think I'll have a 7&7 for a change. In fact"—he reached into his pocket and removed a hundred-dollar bill, slapped it down on the bar's scuffed surface—"get a round for all these folks," he said. "And keep 'em coming."

As Barb worked her way along the rectangular contour of the bar, Bobby noticed Wade Little shooting pool and sharing a pitcher with Gil Cunningham at the other end of the long, narrow room. Roger Kneff sat at a high-top, chalking a cue, waiting to play the winner.

Bobby walked in that direction, plucked a pool cue from the holder by the juke, and went back to the rail of the bar for his 7&7.

As he sipped it, his grip tightened around the cue, his knuckles turning white.

The thought of leaving town entered his head again as he slipped another C-note into Barb's tip jar and began moving back toward them.

Wade and Gil had just finished their game, and Roger was racking a new one.

Bobby's mind divided: thinking of Dee and her unwavering forgiveness of people who didn't deserve it; thinking of himself and how he wasn't sure he'd ever be capable of it himself.

It was apparent that Wade and the others hadn't seen him come in, distracted and drunk on a day's worth of cheap beer and grand gestures.

He approached the three men, whose backs were turned, and Bobby knew he had again come to that place where the road split in two directions. His hand squeezed the cue, the sweat from his palm making it slick in his grasp. He sipped the 7&7 once more before setting it on the corner of an empty table. His mind grew quiet then. He heard the ice shift in the glass. Louder than everything else, even the sound of his own beating heart.

The Thirteenth Step

Wednesday night and I'm in the back making coffee while out front Rico moves in on some new girl, subtle as a swooping vulture. There's a name for guys like him—Thirteenth Steppers—and meetings are full of them. The girl's probably twenty-two, twenty-three but could be forty. Looks like she's been dragged through the circles of hell and barely lived to tell about it. Hair a nest of scorched red ends and black roots. She doesn't have the bitter eyes and pinched face of someone court ordered, though. She's desperate to make a change.

At least tonight she is.

The coffee urn gurgles like a wheezing lung as I set out the cream and sugar—lots of sugar—and go out to finish setting up: literature table, collection basket, 50/50 tickets, laminated step cards with curled edges. My sponsor told me doing these things would help keep me straight. He called it service. Giving back. But that was before he relapsed and got locked up, so I'm still not sold.

Rico places a hand on the new girl's back, begins the regurgitated litany of maxims and readymade phrases: *Welcome Home. Easy Does It. One Day at a Time. It Works if You Work It.* And so on. They're taped up all over the podium—promises for a better way of life.

But some of us are still waiting for the Awakening. To become *Happy, Joyous,* and *Free.* A day at a time. Still waiting.

I've been keeping busy like I was told. A meeting a day, sometimes more if I get time off at the carwash because of rain. I was told, *You drank every day, you need a meeting every day.* What I wasn't told was for how long—how long until such dedication bears fruit.

Before, I was rarely ever at home, and when I was, I still wasn't, not really. That's what my wife used to say. And she was right about that. The irony is I'm still hardly there. "You've traded hanging out with drunks for hanging out with drunks," she tells me damn near every night when I come strolling in around eleven. And of course, she's still right.

Last week she asked me, "Those meetings—how long are they supposed to last usually?"

"About an hour," I said.

She looked at the clock on the wall beside the fridge. "You've been gone four."

"That's just the meeting," I said. "There's more to it than that. You've got to set up and tear down, meet people, build a support system." What I didn't tell her is that I no longer have a sponsor, and instead of engaging in fellowship afterward, I drive around town, past old haunts, sometimes

132

park and sit for hours outside a bar or a liquor store just to see how long until I cave.

"Uh-huh," she said. "And this?" She gestured around the room, the piled up laundry and dirty dishes, then picked up a stack of unpaid bills. "And these?"

"Donna, I'm tryin' real hard," I said.

"You want support, fine," she said. "But I could use a little myself, dammit."

As she walked out of the room, it occurred to me that nothing's really changed except now I remember things in the morning and don't wake up with broken bones and blood on my clothes. There's still this distance, and no matter how many drinks I don't take I can't close the gap. There's no longer anything to blur the damage I've caused, and the more clear-headed I am, the more I'm forced to see.

I've put her through a lot. Can't even count the number of times she had to stop me from pissing in the pantry or taking a shit in the clothes hamper.

One of my last blackouts, I came to around noon the next day. Bedroom door in splintered fragments all over the hall floor. My knuckles gashed and swollen. She'd been fixing me some food to help soak up the booze I'd been swimming in since breakfast when I passed out. She tried to wake me and I flipped, went through the door like a rabid ape. Then I went outside and beat the hell out of our charcoal grill with a lead pipe until it was nothing but a dented heap of scrap. Woke up the entire neighborhood. I didn't remember any of it, but the evidence was all there. Like the path of destruction in the wake of a tornado. And all because she wanted to love my sorry ass.

#

Some guy from out of town, an old ex-marine named Mitch, is sharing his story. Rico keeps getting up to get the new girl more coffee. He sits really close to her, staring at her tits and whispering in her ear as she sips from the paper cup clutched between her shaky palms. She looks uncomfortable, but occasionally smiles at something he says. A smile that looks false and out of options.

Mitch says he was dishonorably discharged and almost sent to federal prison for selling stolen assault rifles on the streets of DC before he got sober. "I'm an alcoholic of the truly hopeless variety," he tells the room, and from the looks of his burst capillaries and drifting right eye, that much is probably true. "If I couldn't get my hands on any whiskey, I'd mix up some canned heat, and that'd be good enough for me," he says." I've heard of guys doing this. Strain Sterno gel through an old sock or a loaf of bread to extract the ethanol. Bowery bums call it *squeeze*. Tastes like hell and rots the optic nerve, but they say it works in a pinch. "In the end, I stumbled into a pharmacy and guzzled a bottle of aftershave before the cops finally showed up," he says. "By then my organs were shuttin' down and I'd lost the sight in one eye." He leans over the podium, and scans the room, his right eye like a loose ball bearing rattling around in his skull.

After the "What It's Like Now" segment of Mitch's lead, he takes a seat while this month's chairperson, Eileen, thanks him for sharing his experience, strength, and hope with us, then presents him with a Xeroxed certificate which was passed around and signed like a Get Well card.

Eileen's a spitfire. Can't seem to open her mouth without letting you know just how far down the scale she'd gone before arriving here. "They used to call me 'Eileen the Blowjob Queen,'" she tells everyone she meets in the rooms, as if this amount of disclosure will put their minds at ease. Her personal end of the road was some fleabag motel in West Virginia. She'd held up a liquor store, smoked a bunch of rock, and had a shootout with the police for over an hour before she ran out of bullets. The incident was on the show *Cops*, which makes her the closest thing to a celebrity most of us will ever meet. Now Eileen runs her own appliance rental and repo business and is working on a master's degree in business or accounting or something like that. She's one of the successes, I guess.

Men and women aren't supposed to sponsor each other for obvious reasons, but Eileen's the only person I've met since mine went off the rails that I can take seriously, who doesn't seem to be putting on a show or looking for praise. The new girl would be in good hands with her. But when I look across the room after the raffle and the Lord's Prayer, the table where she and Rico were sitting is empty.

Before clearing the tables and putting up the chairs, I check outside, where several people stand around smoking, drinking coffee, and telling war stories. In the parking lot, the new girl climbs into a car driven by an old woman who looks like she could be her grandmother. Rico bends down and smiles at the old woman through the passenger window. He nods. *No, the pleasure is all mine,* the nod says. *She'll be fine. We take care of each other here.* He jots something down on a scrap of paper, then hands it to the girl and makes a gesture. *Call me.*

He watches as they drive away. When he turns to walk toward his car, he sees me looking and smiles the innocent smile of a kid caught with his hand in the cookie jar. The parking lot lights shimmer off his greasy bald scalp, his gold chain twinkles and gleams. As he moves, his nylon track suit whispers *hush* with each step he takes.

#

Driving home, I think about the old marine drinking Sterno squeeze like some Depression wino, about how, during those last six months or so, my wife had begun to wonder where all her baking extracts had gone and why she had to buy a new bottle of Listerine every week.

"I had the freshest breath in town," I sometimes joke. You can do that after a while. Hindsight has a way of bringing out the humor in certain things, if you let it.

But Donna has yet to laugh.

"I don't see what's so damn funny about it," she says any time I try to lighten the mood by joking about the time I puked all over her nice down comforter and blamed it on the cat. Or the time I fell asleep on the john, pants down and the door wide open at our son's sixth birthday party. Or when I tackled that animated Halloween store dummy after I triggered the motion sensor and thought it was waving a knife at me.

"It's important to be able to laugh at yourself," I tell her on these occasions. "It's part of the recovery process."

"Yeah," she says, "you keep saying that."

#

Rico used to manage a strip club, Mustang Sally's out on Route 7. He dealt dope to the dancers and arranged escorts for old men and truckers on the sly. When the owner caught wind of it and canned him, Rico took his business, as well as some of the girls he'd hooked, over to the South Side and started running them out of a bar called The Sundown.

My lust for strange women is one of my many shortcomings, so I've heard some things. Like how he stakes out the meetings over at the recovery clinic, offers rides to girls fresh out of treatment, clean but still mixed up in the head. Gives them free dope before past experience reminds them there's no such thing.

Rico glosses over that part of his story during the Saturday evening panel discussion at Fellowship Hall. Might make him look bad in front of the new girl, who finally stood and introduced herself at the beginning of the meeting: *Hi, I'm Nikki, alcoholic addict.*

The way *he* tells it, he was up to a gallon of bottom-shelf gin a day before his broken spirit just couldn't take any more. "I had a spiritual malady," he says, looking down at his laced fingers and shaking his head. "But now I got a program, thanks to my Higher Power." He points a gold-ringed finger toward the ceiling. "I got to hit my knees first thing in the morning and last thing at night and pray for that strength." He looks up and there's a collective nod. "Got to turn my will over and give freely to others what was freely given." There's a murmuring assent.

It could be any one of them up there talking. They all sound the same, every damn one.

Nikki's sitting in the far corner near the exit. She still looks weathered, out of her element—*You and me both,* I think—but she looks better than she did on Wednesday. She's got a new dye job. Copper waves and frosted tips. Face a shade brighter, as if someone has nudged a dimmer switch somewhere inside her. The ash-gray motes around her eyes have faded a bit. It could just as likely be the makeup, though. An illusion.

She looks in my direction, and I offer a nod, a casual smile. She smiles back. For a moment that smile gets me thinking about the things I could do to her, that we could do to each other. The urges we could foster. The sorrows we could subdue. But with no chemical buffer between these thoughts and my desire to be decent, the moment passes quickly, and I only feel disgusted with myself.

When the discussion is over, Rico returns to the table where Nikki is sitting. He's done a good job keeping her isolated, even in these crowded rooms. Always whispering in her ear or pointing out something on the meeting schedule, something in the Big Book. Some disapproving glances, but no one ever says anything. It's typical. Pay lip service to the program, then turn a blind eye when shit gets shady. Seems to be the common approach. Less than a year in and I've figured out this much.

Of course, these are the kinds of things I'm supposed to work through with my sponsor—reservations, resentments, the bondage of self. But even if mine didn't jumped ship, I suspect I'd have my doubts.

I try to tell myself, Maybe you should stop thinking so damn much. It's rarely done you any good. Take your own inventory. His business is none of yours. But when I see them get into his Jag after the meeting lets out—Nikki in a pair of tight black pants and spiked heels, Rico in his gators and creased jeans—I decide that on second thought, maybe it is.

#

When it comes to righting one's wrongs, making amends, some are easier than others. Paying off outstanding debts, for instance. Depending on the amount, it might take some time, but it's straight forward. When it's done, it's done. Some bridges stay burned, and that's just how it goes. But it's the emotional wreckage of those close to you— sometimes it seems there's no fixing that.

My wife and son should have been first on the list, always, but they're more than just names to scratch a line through. Apologies become empty phrases, and I've done little to *show* them I've changed. And how can I?

139

Donna, she still cries in her sleep. Things I've said and done etched so deep she can't escape them even in her dreams: the women, the lies, the broken doors.

And my boy, T.J.—he's nine years old and looks at me like I'm a stranger, someone he's afraid to be left alone with. Ruined birthdays and Christmas mornings. I showed up to his school talent show drunk last year and started shouting obscenities at a young girl who laughed at him when he went on stage. I was escorted out by several big ass motherfuckers. He still gets picked on because of it, gets off the bus every day looking like he's carrying the whole cruel world on his back.

How the hell do you make up for something like that?

#

Avoiding home, I follow them from the meeting to The Sundown, sit in my pickup and wait for them to come out. They exit the bar about an hour after going in, and Nikki can barely stand. Rico's got an arm around her as he talks on his cell and guides her toward the Jag.

Following, I hang back.

He makes two stops. First, JQ's drive-thru on South and Judson. Five blocks north, a seedy three-story Foursquare with a slanted porch and blacked out windows. Security cameras hanging from the peeling eaves. Pit bull pacing the front yard at the end of a fat chain.

For several minutes, they just sit in the car with the headlights off, then Rico gets out and goes around to the side of the house. A minute or two and he's back in the car, rolling slow.

He glides and weaves into the Valley, over Center Street Bridge and across the river. East Side, creeping along cracked and sloped streets. Haselton, La La Land, Plaza View Projects, The Brooks. Dodge City—not a nice place to call home.

I'm with them, a block back, until they turn onto a weedy strip of pavement and park beside a darkened bungalow. The street's a dead end. Just a guardrail, some chain link with tangled trees reaching through it. Idling at a gang-tagged stop sign, I watch as Rico guides Nikki from behind, hands on her hips, toward the front door. Several minutes later: the glow of candlelight guttering through an upstairs curtain.

When after a while they don't emerge, I tell myself, *Do something*, and in the same breath, *Why bother? Who's to say she's not where she wants to be?* But that's bullshit, and I know it. A convenience. A choice made in such a state isn't a choice. *Still, what the hell are you gonna to do about it?*

A light rain stipples my windshield as I grip the truck's door handle and imagine myself going in there, trying to save the day like some unarmed Charles Bronson wannabe. Getting myself opened up in the dark by who knows who.

But like you said, you don't know what she wants. And that's true. That's true.

The rain gains weight, fat drops slashing through slanting lamplight, and I say it out loud: "You don't know what she wants." And I reply: "True. That's true." I say it again and again as I drive home, as if repetition will convince me.

#

Wednesday night and I'm in the back making coffee while out front Rico chitchats with a couple fly-by-nights who pop in once in a while. When he spots another new girl and zeros in, the two guys do the old nudge-and-wink and go outside to smoke. This girl, a tiny blonde with wrecked written all over her, is wrapped in the same veil of desperation that Nikki was and stands on the same high ledge.

Nikki hasn't been with Rico at any of the regular meetings this week: Sunday Night Sanity Seekers, Monday's Drop the Rock, the Tuesday night 12&12—not a single one. That's because Sunday morning a young black girl, leaving for church with her family, discovered the overdosed body of a young white woman splayed in the grass outside her bedroom window in The Brooks. Left there like a sack of trash. All of two sentences in Monday's paper. Nothing but a footnote in a larger narrative no one wants to read.

No name was given, so I don't know for certain that it was her—*maybe not,* I tell myself—but that's what I believe. Because that's how fast it can happen. One day you're in and one day you're out, and if you're lucky you're not out for good.

I followed Rico again on Sunday, on Monday, on Tuesday, because I couldn't stop thinking about it, about her. Can't.

He's kept the same routine: The Sundown—up the rickety staircase around back and into the apartment above the bar. Goes in alone, comes out twenty minutes later with some other limp Nikki shuffling at his side. Next: JQ's and the house five blocks up before zig-zagging his way to the East Side. Same house, same forgotten neighborhood.

The nights have tumbled into one another, following and thinking and following and thinking. And as I've laid on the couch early into the morning, running through it all while my wife cries into her pillow in the other room, while my son nurtures his quiet hatred of me, I've hardly slept for knowledge of Nikki's fate.

So now, when Rico gets up to hit the restroom, I seize the opportunity and introduce this newcomer to Eileen, who offers the girl, Mandy, a cigarette.

"Tommy," Eileen says. I look and she nods toward the brewing coffee urn. I nod back, and when the coffee's ready, I bring them each a cup loaded with cream and sugar. As I'm walking away, I hear Eileen say, "Honey, there ain't nothing you done, nothing you can say that'll shock me. You know what they used to call me? Used to call me 'Eileen the Blowjob Queen.'" That gets a smile out of the girl, and it's enough that I think maybe she has a chance.

When Rico returns from the restroom, he doesn't look happy when he sees Mandy making friends, but he doesn't

143

interfere. Throughout the rest of the meeting, I watch him watching her. Tonight's speaker is one of those old-timer windbags that likes to quote from the Big Book like a preacher reciting bible verses: page numbers and entire paragraphs from memory. It's the kind of pretentious proselytizing that impresses some people, but not me. Each time he launches into one of his "The Big Book tells us" spiels, I busy my mind with anything I can to keep from listening.

But there's only one thing on my mind.

Rico sits there mean mugging Eileen but trying not to be obvious about it. When the meeting is over, some people disperse while others linger, like me, afraid to go home and face the rubble that still remains under their own roofs.

Eileen invites me to join her, Mandy, and a few others for coffee at the Idle Hour Diner.

"Thanks," I say, "but I'll take a rain check." Outside these rooms—hell, even inside—I still have trouble socializing when I'm sober, even after almost a year. It's one of the drawbacks of getting carried away so young, never learning how to engage in basic human interactions.

Rico watches them all piling into their cars with a scowl on his face, lips drawn tight, jaw clenched. I'd like to say it feels good to see him like this, for him to not know that I know, if no one else seems to, what he's all about. And perhaps it does. Perhaps it also feels good to know that now a girl might make it. But what's that worth, really? There will be others, and even the ones who manage to dodge the Ricos of the world have to choose sooner or later. And right choices are hard for people like us. Any fool will tell you.

#

This spring has been a wet one, and I've been lucky to clock maybe twenty hours a week at the Wash & Wax. Today's fair but slow. I'm toweling off a cherry-red Audi sedan and keep seeing the last month or so playing in its shiny surface: Rico and Nikki and dark roads leading to dark houses. And the last year: clusters of disconsolate faces filling church basements and union halls waiting to be freed, nodding to lies and nodding to lies and nodding until they believe, until they can embrace the things they've done, finally close their eyes and sleep; my sponsor's mugshot in the local paper; the taunting lure of neon lights; Donna and T.J. and the bitter memories that float around inside them; days stacked on days stacked on days of thinking *this is it, this is it, this is how it ends*, not with a bang or a whimper but a cold and stunning silence.

#

It's not that late, only 8:30, but I've been gone all day. When I walk in, T.J. retreats into his video games and my wife retreats to the bedroom. They don't have to grant me forgiveness, I remind myself. But hopefully someday they will. Hopefully, I'll soon learn to show them I've changed.

Hopefully, I have.

Though I've received my one-year coin, and though there are some who walk the talk, my faith in the program is tenuous at best. I see wolves and I see sheep and I see that we're all of us one or the other. I see that you can change all the aspects of your life that they say to change—people, places, and things—but our natures are seldom overcome. If I make it till midnight, I'll have another twenty-four hours under my belt. One more day of walking a straight line on solid ground to show for a lifetime lost at sea. One more day stacked on another. Maybe one closer to serenity.

But as I sit in the kitchen, in darkness save for the hall light pooling on the floor, I stare at the book in front of me, the one that's supposed to have all the answers, and know that some things wrecked can't be salvaged. I place an ashtray on top of it and watch it fill. The hours pass. I picture the suspicion in my wife's eyes each night when I return home, each night when I run out of reasons not to. She hasn't said it but hasn't needed to—her silence so much louder than words.

She thinks I'm back on the bottle. And with a growing dread that I'll never be absolved, I begin to think that maybe I should be.

The Nest, the Cage

Hey Ma,

I just tried to call but there was no answer. You must be working. Sorry I haven't called or written in a while. Hope you haven't been worried. They just let me out of the hole this morning, but before you get all worked up just know that I'm fine. It was just some young punk in the chow hall, didn't like that I wouldn't give him an extra heel of bread while I was working the line. That's why I hate working in there. Always someone wanting extra and getting pissed off when they can't get it. We ended up having some words and next thing you know I'm sitting solo in the hole for thirty days. They take away all your privileges, no phone calls, no mail, no nothing except you in a small room wondering if it's gonna cost you your early release. So that's why you haven't heard from me, if you've been wondering.

Anyway, thanks a lot for the food box and the books and envelopes. It was real nice to come back into Gen Pop and have some things to help me through. Lately the eighteen dollars state pay I get is gone before I get it because of owing for things fronted on the two-for-one (it's an interest rate thing). I'd been saving up the envelopes you've sent along with your letters, but to be honest I've traded a lotta those for cigarettes. It's crazy. Never woulda thought you could use some things for money, but next to coffee and tobacco, envelopes are like gold in here.

It seems like longer than it's been since we talked. I hope when you didn't hear from me you didn't drive all the way down and then have to turn around and leave because I couldn't have any visitors. I wanted to call and tell you not to come, but like I said, they wouldn't let me use the phone. And I'm sure no one called you to let you know. They don't tell us anything. Like last month when you couldn't make it down to visit because of the roads. No one even told me if you'd called or anything, just left me sitting and waiting. It didn't surprise me though. You know there was this old dude, Mr. Pope, a couple months back he asked to go to the infirmary because he was having some kind of chest pains, but every CO he asked just told him to get his ass back on his bunk. And you know what? The next morning they found him dead of a heart attack. I shit you not. That's how they do people in here. And you know what else? They get away with it. But I probably shouldn't be telling you these things, because I know how you worry. I try not to tell you certain things as I'm sure you know.

Anyway, that was a bummer you couldn't make the drive. But I understand. It's just that couple hours with you every month is the only thing I really have to look forward to in here since I still haven't heard from Brenda. Have you heard from her? She hasn't replied to any of my letters and hasn't answered my calls. Probably can't afford it. How much is Global Tel Link costing you? I hope it's not too much. I stopped writing to Brenda though, because when she doesn't reply, well, you know how I can get. I start getting mad and saying things I shouldn't like if she wasn't always on my case maybe I wouldn't have done what I done and be in this joint right now. But it's not her fault. I know that. It's just every time I sit down to write her a letter that's what it turns into. I'm thinking maybe she's really had it with me this time, Ma. And can I be mad about it, really? I mean, I love her and little Casey more than life and miss them so much it's an actual pain I feel on the daily. Have you ever missed someone so bad it physically hurt? I always thought stuff like that was just talk. It really does hurt though. But was I thinking of them when we were together? Hell, maybe they'd be better off without me if I'm honest about it right now. Anyway, if I get tossed in the hole again I'll probably lose my slim shot at Judicial Release come spring, if I haven't lost it already.

It's not like I go looking for trouble, Ma, but you know it always has a way of finding me somehow. Been that way ever since I was a snot-nose kid. Remember when I was in kindergarten and blew up that sewer drain on the playground after dumping in a can of stuff I found by the dumpster then throwing in a lit match from the book I swiped from your purse? I still don't know what was in that can. But I do know that fat ogre Miss Shaw had it out for me from then on. Hard to believe I can't remember names of some people from last week, but I remember that miserable woman from almost thirty years ago. Did I ever tell you she put charcoal in my Christmas stocking? Right before the holiday she had all us kids make stockings out of construction paper and yarn, and when we came back to school, they were all filled with candy except mine and this other kid, Michael something, I think. Ours were stuffed with actual charcoal. Can you believe that?

Don't know why I'm even bringing it up other than to say maybe I was always bound to be locked up in a place like this. You think that could be true? Like maybe deep down I knew it even then, so I just went ahead and lived a certain kind of way that was just following the path fate had laid out in front of me. You think a five-year-old could think something like that? Of course I don't remember, but I think maybe I did know. I'm sure Miss Shaw knew. She knew and let me know I wouldn't amount to much more than that. That a piece of coal was the peak of what I'd ever become. Maybe she was right.

I guess I've had lots of time for thinking on these kinds of things. Especially in the hole. Gen Pop is so much better because there's more to do and the time goes by faster. In the hole it's just you and the toilet and the four walls really close together and no real sense of time passing. A day can feel like a week and a month has been enough to drive some guys crazy. They come out looking dazed and deprived. Even I felt a little strange outside on the yard after having no fresh air or natural light for so long. First thing I noticed was how the sky seemed bigger than usual. But really it wasn't so bad. Some guys cope with it better than others I guess, and it's a good thing I mostly like being alone. It did get tough this last time though because we didn't get to visit before I went in. And like I said they don't let you have anything in there. You only got yourself for company and that's almost never a good thing because the person you were and are, and the person you want to be all get to bickering and there's not much to shut them up once they get going. And to be honest, I've been worrying a little myself about what's gonna happen.

One of the things that helped me through was just knowing that when they let me out maybe there'd be a letter from you waiting for me, or that I'd get to call, or you'd be coming to visit soon. I don't like to admit it, but this last hole shot got to me so that I've pretty much given up on Brenda ever writing or answering the phone. In the least I'd like to hear my daughter's voice. I know it's only been a year, but that's a long time when it comes to not seeing or hearing your own child. Sometimes I wonder if Dad ever felt like I'd just forget he existed somewhere just because he was gone before you had me. Pretty much I have. But now that I got a kid of my own, all I can think is how I wanna be there, ya know? Maybe you could get ahold of Brenda, get a recent picture of my baby girl for me. Brenda always did like you and I know she'd still want you to be in Casey's life even if she doesn't want me in it. God, what if I really did mess it all up this time around, Ma?

I imagine Casey's gotten so big already. I bet she looks more and more like her mama every day too. She always did have Brenda's big eyes and sweet smile. Hair looking like it was brushed by a windstorm. Have you seen her at all? I'm afraid I'll forget what she looks like before too long, even more that she's already forgotten me. I know that's probably over dramatic, but a guy worries about these things. I think I heard once kids don't really remember things from that young. I hope that's not true. She's only two, Ma. You think she remembers me at all? Maybe she'll be like you, like when you told me once about how you still remember sounds and lights around you from right after you were born and your legs were all twisted and they had to put casts on them so they'd grow proper, how you told me you remember the room and the tools being dropped onto a tray or something. I hope Casey has a good memory like that, at least when it comes to her daddy and the times she was happy.

One of the things I've been most worrying about though is that Brenda's gonna take my girl somewhere where I can't never find her. But even if she doesn't, even if she sticks by me like she's always done, through interventions and house arrest and months here and there in jail, this time we have Casey, and I'll have missed so much of her growing up that maybe I'll just be a stranger and never get that time back that I've thrown away. And that's what I've done, I know. What I've been doing since I can remember. Throwing time away. And I know no matter what happens to me, if I get out in April or do my whole five, or worse . . . I won't get that time back. I'll never be able to fill the space hollowed out by my not being there, the space in me, and maybe in her. If she remembers.

Do you think I should write to her? I've thought about it, but Brenda would probably just rip it up. Ever since my first go at rehab I've thought about writing my baby girl and telling her about me, so she doesn't have to hear it from someone else. I could tell her everything, but maybe that's a bad idea, telling a little kid her daddy robbed someone to get high instead of being home with her like he shoulda been.

Maybe there's a better way of saying it. I don't know. Maybe I will write her. I could send the letters to you and you could keep them for her for when she's older maybe. Would you do that, just in case something happens?

You're probably wondering what I mean by "something." It's just this last mix up was worse than the others, Ma. Like there might be more trouble maybe. The kid from the chow hall ended up in the infirmary and I still don't know what happened to him after that. He was hurt pretty bad. But it was him or me and that's just the truth of it. Anyway, there's a chance I could get another charge, but don't freak out just yet. It might be nothing. And if nothing comes of it, I'm seriously thinking of trying to get transferred to another facility, maybe something closer to you so you wouldn't have to drive so far when you visit. Or if not that maybe to another unit at least. Back to the one I was in before. They got me in 4-house again now, which is where they put everyone when they get out of the hole. And everyone fresh off the bus. They call it the gutter because it's full of young hard asses, not much more than boys most of them, ones that are like second or third generation gangbangers in on their second or third of a lifelong run of state numbers and short time bits for slinging dope or shooting up some corner store. They're in earning reputations and don't care about a damn thing. They're living in here like it's out there, strong arming new guys for their commissary and whatever else they can take. Testing you to see if you're gonna last. It's sorta funny (not really) but we're not that different. After all, I'm here now for taking what didn't belong to me, right?

I've tried to mind my own, Ma, I promise you I have. I've tried to finish this time quick and quiet, but there's always someone with something to prove and then you're in it, and it is what it is until it isn't. Until maybe it's something else. Like years added on to your bit. That's how it works. I'm no saint, you and me both know that, but what's a guy supposed to do? Just let some dude come up on him and take a swing and not swing back? I mean, it's not like I caught him in the shower with a padlock in a sock or anything. But he wouldn't let it go, and all over a piece of damn bread. Hell, if I'd have known it would turn out this way, that I'd catch a couple stitches and maybe another case for it, I'd have given the little punk the whole damn loaf.

Anyway, Ma, I just want you to know that I don't know what's gonna happen. I don't know just how bad I hurt him. I'm told he's connected, though, which in here means if it's not him the next time it'll be someone else. That's the way it works. I really am hoping I didn't hurt him worse than I think. Since getting out of the hole all I've been able to do besides write this letter is wait to be called in front of the sergeant or worse the warden. Have them tell me to get comfortable because I just bought myself another trip in front of the judge, maybe another three or five years to run concurrently. That'd be just my luck, wouldn't it? So far nothing, but this place is only so big, and it's only a matter of time before something.

But like I said, I don't mean to upset you. I just figure you should know is all. That I might be here longer than I thought. Or maybe a lot less. I'll try to keep you posted. I'll probably even call before you get this, but if you don't hear from me, try not to worry. Just look in on my baby girl if you can and try to get that picture of her for me.

Sorry if I got to rambling or repeating myself. It's just that I sometimes forget what all I've told you before and what I haven't. I think I'm better at getting things out on paper than when we talk because no matter how glad I am to see you during our visits I can't help but watch the clock on the wall and know that our time together will soon be over. I know your trips to see me are a burden. I know they're hard for you to manage money-wise and all. And I know it's hard for you to see me in here. But it means more than you'll ever know that you haven't turned your back on me.

Bye, Ma. Love and miss you.

Yours always,

-Dustin

P.S.

Maybe you could do me one more thing? When you see my baby girl, maybe you can tell her some of the good things about me. Like about when I was little and would sit in the crook behind your knees whenever you laid on your side, how we called it your nest, and you were like a mother bird and I was your chick or whatever. How we'd watch old movies together like that until I fell asleep there. I bet you thought I forgot about that. But I never did. I've been thinking about it a lot actually. I've been thinking about how bad I wish I was still that kid, even for just a little while, in your nest on the daybed in our tiny little apartment, maybe already doomed but maybe not completely. Maybe not yet bound for a cage. Back when there was still a chance. Maybe you can make a nest for my baby girl and tell her stories about when you were little. Tell her you'll keep her safe like you always did me. She'll like that.

-D

Portraits of the Dead and Dying

Dwight had just torn open the pack of Lucky Strikes he'd stolen from Mort's Little Shopper when we saw the plane going down. We were in the patch of woods behind St. John's, where we liked to horse around on those long summer afternoons when our mothers were working, and our fathers were laid off and either slouched in front of the TV or down at Miller's Tap tying one on.

"Holy Shit!" Dwight said. "You see that?"

The plane was one of those Cessna puddle jumper deals, looked like the piece-together toys they had over at the discount drugstore where my mom bought her make-up and my old man's stomach medicine. It came arcing across the sky in a spiraling nosedive. Dwight jammed the pack of smokes into the pocket of his Rustlers and shouted, "Come on!"

Our bikes were lying in the grass behind the church pavilion, and as we started down the hill toward the road, the plane disappeared behind a barn at the old Anders dairy farm just outside of town. A moment after it dropped out of sight, we heard the crash, such a faint sound, you probably wouldn't hear it at all if you didn't know it was coming.

Pedaling out Main Street, to where it was no longer Main but a two-lane highway leading into Pennsylvania, I did my best to keep up with Dwight. He was more excited than I'd ever seen him. We were twelve and thirteen years old, Dwight being the older of us, and the most excitement we knew besides setting fire to anthills, pissing from the turnpike overpass onto passing cars, and smoking behind the church came from the small wall of VHS tapes at the corner store.

"Maybe it's bank robbers," Dwight said, out of breath.

"Really?"

"Or maybe it's the Russians."

"You really think so?"

The previous weekend, Dwight and I had watched this movie where Communists invaded a small town out west somewhere, and though I knew it wasn't real, I was nervous as we skidded to a stop at the crest of the rutted dirt road, stirring up dust.

"Could be," he said.

We were on the far edge of the old farm, which I'd overheard my old man say had gone under, something to do with the bank coming in and making everybody leave. The land had been empty for a couple years, and now the fields were overgrown with nettle and choked with briar. We sat there on our bikes, looking down into a grassy hollow. Just us for at least two miles in any direction. Nothing else around but rolling, scrubby fields and sun-parched dirt.

Before I knew it, Dwight was at the bottom of the hollow, off his bike and running toward the downed plane. Close up, it reminded me even more of a broken toy, maybe thrown to the ground by God Himself. Seeing it made me feel small, and as I coasted down to join him, and the land rose around me, I swore the earth was about to swallow me whole.

The tail of the plane had busted off along with one of its wings. They were strewn across the ground with a bunch of smaller pieces. We discovered the pilot was the only one inside, still strapped in to his seat with a piece of crooked metal poking out of his chest. He wasn't moving.

Dwight's face was alit with joy. "This is the greatest thing's ever happened to us, Jesse. Don't you think so?"

I wasn't certain, but I agreed that it was. "You think he's dead?"

"Sure looks like it," he said.

"Maybe we should touch his neck."

Dwight looked at me sideways. "Why the hell would we wanna do that?"

"I don't know. That's what they always do in the movies. You know, to check and see if they're still alive?"

"I ain't touching his neck. You touch his neck."

"But I don't know how to do it," I said.

"Me neither." Dwight picked up a small metal rod that had detached from somewhere on the plane and poked the pilot in the neck. "How's that?"

The man didn't budge, so Dwight poked him some more, all the while repeating, "This is the greatest thing's ever happened to us."

#

There was nothing inside the plane besides a tool box, some parachute packs and helmets, and a Styrofoam cooler that had busted apart and spilled empty beer cans all over the small cabin.

"Damn," Dwight said, looking disappointed. "I was really hoping it'd be bank robbers."

Picking up one of the packs, I said, "These parachutes are pretty neat, though."

"Yeah, but what are we gonna do with those, dumbass? It's not like we can use them or nothin'." He climbed back toward the front and began going through the dead pilot's pockets.

"What are you doing?"

He found the man's wallet and removed a sheaf of bills. "The hell's it look like? He don't need it no more."

"Yeah, I guess not," I said, and wondered what the punishment might be for stealing from the dead.

Dwight went through the rest of the wallet, tossing bits of paper and plastic cards over his shoulder. "Woo hoo, check it out," he said, and handed me a faded photograph with ragged edges. It was of a dark-skinned woman with narrow eyes, lying on a mattress in a pair of skimpy red underwear and nothing else. She was young and pretty like the women in the magazines I'd found stashed in my old man's tool shed, but I thought she also looked a little sad.

He snatched back the photo and grinned, exposing a mouthful of crooked teeth. "Man, I'd lay some serious pipe in that," he said.

Now I was pretty sure he didn't know what laying pipe meant any more than I did, only that his old man, Lefty, was always saying it about girls on the TV, but I nodded just the same and said, "Hell yeah."

After staring at the woman for another minute or so, Dwight pulled out the pack of Luckies, tucked the photo inside, and put it back in his pocket. "Maybe I'll let you borrow her sometime," he said, and slugged me in the arm. Then he started going through the pilot's pockets again.

There was a chrome flask in the man's inside jacket pocket. Dwight unscrewed the cap, sniffed it, and took a small swig. His face went a little funny after that, but he managed to swallow. He winced and coughed. "Damn, that's good stuff," he said. "Wanna try some?"

I smelled that flammable smell coming off Dwight and thought about my old man sitting at home, probably already half in the bag. "No, thanks," I said.

Whatever was in it must not have been as good as he claimed, because Dwight put the flask back and continued searching the man's jacket.

"We should probably get out of here," I said.

Dwight ignored me. "Aw cool," he said, holding up a Zippo lighter with an eagle and an American flag engraved on the side of it. He took out the pack of Luckies again and lit one. After a few drags, he said, "Here," and counted out twenty dollars. "You get half. But I get to keep the lighter."

#

Though I wasn't sure just how long we'd been there, by the time we climbed out of the plane the sun had begun inching toward the horizon. It was probably six o'clock by then, but it was July, so it would still be hours before dark. As we stood among the wreckage, I was even more eager to get the hell away from there. And Dwight finally agreed. Then, as we were getting ready to ride back home, we heard something, a low moaning coming from about a hundred yards off.

"Shhh," Dwight said. "What's that?"

"I don't know. It's coming from over that way."

We crept in the direction of the sound and found a man laid out in a clump of tall weeds, his body tangled up in the lines of his parachute. He wore a helmet and goggles, but his head looked like it was screwed on wrong. One of his arms was bent in a way it shouldn't have been, and a fractured bone stuck out through one of his legs just above the knee.

"Whoa," I said, unable to think of anything else.

"Yeah," Dwight said. "Maybe you should touch his neck." He laughed, his excitement restored.

The man's eyes were rolled back in their sockets, and the sounds he was making reminded me of the ones my old man made between heaves as he wretched over the porch rail after too much of the hard stuff.

"We should probably call for help," I said.

"You see a goddamn phone anywhere?"

"We could go back to town, tell somebody."

"No way," Dwight said, shaking his head.

"But he's still alive."

"Not for much longer, it don't look like." He slugged me in the shoulder again, hard this time. "Check his pockets."

I looked at him. "You serious?"

"Go on," he said, "I did the last one."

I hesitated, not much liking the idea, but went ahead with it anyway.

All the man had on him was a wallet. Inside was about fifty bucks, which, added to the forty we'd already split, was a rather small fortune to us at the time. The man's Ohio State driver's license read Carl Brenton. It occurred to me then that in Dwight's eagerness, he'd probably tossed the pilot's ID somewhere in the plane without even noticing what his name was. If he had noticed, he never said, and I hadn't bothered to ask. But this man, the one on the ground before us, was Carl Brenton. And I really wished I didn't know that, because I realized that as soon as I knew his name I couldn't un-know it.

In his wallet, Carl Brenton also had various business cards, a book of matches, and a photograph in a plastic sleeve. Only this photo was different than the one Dwight had found on the pilot. It was picture of a man, a woman, and two young kids, a boy and a girl. A family portrait. Though the resemblance between the man on the ground and the man in the picture was difficult to see just then, it was no doubt the same person. The woman must have been Carl Brenton's wife, I thought, the kids his son and daughter. It seemed strange to me, the way they were posed together, wearing nice clothes and smiling. Why it was strange I didn't quite know right off, just that it was.

The man's moaning had quieted, but he was still struggling to breathe. His chest, which looked sunken on one side, hitched and fell several times, settled, then hitched some more.

Dwight had returned to his bike and was already halfway up the hill when I knelt beside the man. "I'm real sorry, mister," I said. "I bet help will come real soon, though."

Carl Brenton sucked in a ragged breath and let it out in a stuttering wheeze.

"Let's go, shitbird!" Dwight hollered.

164

Standing up, I slid the photo in my pocket and looked at the man one more time. He'd gone silent and still. For a moment, as I pedaled out of the grassy hollow, I thought I heard him moaning again. But I told myself it was just the wind blowing through the hills.

#

Later that night, Dwight called, told me to turn on the 11:00 news.

My mother had come home from work with a migraine and gone straight to bed, and fortunately for us both, my old man had drunk himself stupid by 8:00 and was out cold on the couch by 9:30.

When I flipped on the news, there was a shot showing several ambulances and police cars lined up on the dirt road, and men in uniforms picking through the debris of the shattered plane. The caption at the bottom of the screen read: TWO DEAD IN LORNFIELD TOWNSHIP PLANE CRASH. They must have got there not long after we left, I thought, because it was still daylight.

"They're sayin' they were a couple of old army guys," Dwight said over the line.

According to the news, the men were retired U.S. military. But that was the only information they gave. No family members had yet been reached for comment, so no names or other details were disclosed, but an investigation was underway as to the cause of the crash. That's when I thought about the Styrofoam cooler, all those beer cans inside the plane. The report didn't mention those, though.

"You didn't tell no one, did you?" Dwight asked.

I hadn't, but since coming home, it was all I'd been able to think about—the man's twisted neck, his sick moans, the way his chest seemed to rattle when he breathed.

"No," I said. "Did you?"

"Hell no I didn't."

"Are we gonna?"

"What do you think?" he said. "First thing they'll want to know is why we didn't say somethin' sooner, why we didn't tell nobody."

"I told you we should go for help, remember?"

"Look, forget it," he said. "No use in sayin' anything now, right?" Several seconds of silence and he said it again: "Right?"

Dwight thought just because he was a year older, he got to make the decisions. And although I didn't like the idea of keeping it all inside, and wanted to push back for once, now didn't seem like the time. Besides, if we talked, I might say too much, might spill everything. He knew that and so did I. So he didn't need to worry. I'd picked the pockets of a dying man. A man by the name of Carl Brenton. And I was in no hurry to share that shame with anyone.

"Right," I said.

After I hung up the phone, I walked down the hall to my bedroom, passing by framed photos as I went. For the first time, I noticed there were none of us as a family. One was of my old man in a boat, holding up the record-breaking trout he'd had mounted and hung above the couch. That fish was his proudest accomplishment, but it still hadn't been enough to put a smile on his face. There was one was of my mother when she was maybe eighteen, a large smile, beautiful. Next to it was another one of her, this one taken years later, her expression one of strained contentment and hidden regrets. Another featured my parents at their slapdash wedding, Mom pregnant with me, my old man looking trapped. There were pictures of me as a baby, me as a boy, me in school. We were all there, up on the wall. But we weren't together.

Standing there it hit me, the strangeness I'd felt earlier in the field as I looked at the picture of Carl Brenton and his family.

In my room, I closed the door and lay in the dark. I took out the photo and held it up in the moonlight spilling through the window above my bed.

My old man had woken up, and I could hear him banging around in the kitchen, muttering about being out of beer. A few minutes later my mother was up and then the muttering became arguing. Then shouting.

For a while I just stared at the smiling people in the photo, wondering what the rest of the Brentons' names were as they stared back at me. After a while, with the image fixed

167

in my mind, I closed my eyes and buried my head beneath my pillow. The wind picked up outside and moaned its way across the rolling countryside as I imagined myself there with them. Happy.

Ballad of a Winter Child, 1978

She stood outside his bedroom window, tapping on the glass. He lifted the blinds in sweatpants and no shirt. Stephen Hayward. Such a cute boy, tall and thin with a nice build from chopping wood. His teeth were straight, and his curly brown hair always hung in his eyes, giving him a shy look, like he was hiding from the rest of the world. They had that in common, she thought—neither of them ever came out from behind their walls when people were around, not really. But with each other it was different, always had been.

"Christ, Missy," he said as he lifted the window. "It's freezing out. What are you doing here?"

"Can I come in?"

He stepped out of the way.

Moving around had been hard the last couple months—she got tired so quickly—and she struggled a little as she climbed through. He took her hand and steadied her until she was inside. It was these sorts of little things that made him different from the others.

She was shivering and underdressed in only a knee-length denim skirt with long johns underneath, combat boots, and a baggy sweatshirt. "I just need to warm up a little," she said.

"What's goin' on? You haven't been in school the last couple days."

"Screw that place," she said with what already sounded like wavering conviction. "I turn eighteen in a little over a year, anyway, and Mom's kicking me out the second she can get away with it. Told me so herself."

There were clothes and radio parts and other gadgets scattered around the room. She smiled at Stephen. He was shirtless and suddenly looked embarrassed, picking up a T-shirt off the floor and pulling it on.

"What are you sayin'?" he asked. "What the hell are you gonna do till then?"

There was a knock at the bedroom door.

"Stephen," said the slurred voice of his old man. "Get out here and get these dishes done. Then get your ass out and unload that firewood from the truck."

"Shit," he said, lowering his voice.

She lowered her voice to match his. "Can you meet me at the old school later?"

"Why the hell are you goin' there? Weather's supposed to get nasty soon—like *real* bad from what they're sayin'."

"Just meet me," she said. "If you can, bring some food and blankets? I got some already, but—"

"What? You're not actually stayin' there."

She knew he'd try to talk her out of it, but she'd made up her mind. "Just for a while, till I can figure something else out," she said. "I got into it with Mom again the other night.

170

She's fuckin' lost it, I swear. You know she actually accused me of tryin' to fuck her new boyfriend?"

She stood there a moment longer, then moved toward the window.

"Wait," he said.

"I'll be in the old Home Ec room," she said. "Come as soon as you can."

"Damn it, hold on."

She was halfway out the window. Moving a little better now that she was warm.

"At least put these on." He handed her a knit stocking cap and some gloves.

"Thanks," she said, then climbed out the rest of the way and pulled the hat down over her long red hair. The gloves were too big for her slender hands, but they were soft inside, lined with wool.

She felt him watching her as she followed the snow-lined ditch west toward the abandoned high school. He was sweet, which is why she'd gone to him. He was the one person she knew she could always go to. There had also been Rachel and Katie, her best friends, or so she'd thought. But they wrote her off after that night last spring, when Rachel had stolen her dad's car and got caught. They'd ended up somewhere in the city. An apartment above a bar with some guys from the truck stop. They were drinking and having a good time. But then her friends were gone, and she was having trouble standing, seeing double. There had been three, but it could have been more. She didn't remember much, just blurred faces and slurred words and a weight on top of her, a feeling that she should go, should have gone with her friends, but now they were gone, and she was there under that weight and unable to move.

If she'd just gone home that night instead, things would be different.

She'd done a remarkable job hiding the truth under baggy clothes, something that went mostly unnoticed since the cold weather had come before she really filled out. And even now, she was tiny compared to some she'd seen. She didn't know whose it was. There had been many, that night and many nights before. She didn't even know some of their names. Not that it would matter. She didn't need anyone anyhow. This was her resolve. No one needed to know until they needed to know. She could do this on her own, had done it this long. Stephen would bring her food, more blankets, and she would be thankful. And when she felt it coming, she would . . . what?

Yes, what will you do then? *I'll figure it out on my own.* You should have done that much already. *Yes. But a person does what a person's got to do. That's what they say and that's what I say now. No time like the present. They say that, too, I've heard it.* That's something they say. *Yes. That's something they say. Figure it out. Don't need no one.*

#

He loved her—at least, he thought it was love. No, he was sure of it. Had since they were kids and her parents divorced and her mom and his dad hooked up that couple times after his own mom died. They shared that, the loss of a parent. One dead and one gone who knows where.

They had watched TV and didn't talk much the first time they met. His old man and her mom had gone to drink, left them at the house with frozen dinners and orders to stay out of things while they were gone or else. They were only seven and had no idea what to do besides just stare at the fuzzy TV in silence. But he felt something for her even then, though he couldn't have explained what it was. But now he knew. That's why he was always fighting. Some people just don't know when to keep their mouths shut. That's what he'd told the principal the last time he was kicked out of school.

Stephen thought about her as he finished stacking the wood under the awning by the side door. Wood heat—propane costs too much, his father always said, electric too. "Highway robbery is what it is. Gets so a man can't even keep a goddamn dollar in his pocket."

By the time he was finished, his fingers were numb, and his nose was running.

When he got back inside, the TV was blaring, and he saw that the old man had passed out in his chair while watching an old western flick. Stephen added some logs to the woodstove, waited for them to catch. Then he loaded some food from the pantry into his backpack: canned stew and fruit cocktail, some beef jerky, crackers, and a pack of chocolate chip cookies. He also grabbed some bologna from the fridge. His father would notice it was gone, but he didn't care. The sonofabitch had made a good wage at the mill before it closed. Black Monday, they'd called it. It was happening to more and more folks these days. And some were saying it was only the beginning. For the last four months he'd collected unemployment. Meanwhile, Stephen chipped in raking leaves and shoveling snow—whatever he could do to bring in a little extra. The food was just as much his, he told himself, and as an afterthought, he filled a small mason jar with some of his father's bourbon, screwed the lid tight, and added it to the bag.

The old man was snoring. He stirred when Stephen accidentally let the cupboard door slam shut, but he didn't wake up.

In his room, Stephen gathered some thermals, pants and shirts, anything else warm. He wrapped it all in his sleeping bag, a thick one he'd saved up for, goose down, good for camping in the cold.

Then he left through his window, so as not to wake his father.

He would stay with her if she wanted, but he knew she'd tell him, *No, go home*. She cared for him, he knew she did, but she had her own way of dealing with things.

He followed the ditch toward the old high school, his boots crunching through the dry crust of snow. The sky was clear, and a pregnant moon hovered above the distant ridge

174

beyond the frozen vein of Trapper's Creek. The moon's cold light spread across the white field, making it sparkle, the snow a long mirror reflecting the stars.

She trusted him enough not to tell anyone where she was. She wouldn't have come to him otherwise, wouldn't have asked for him to meet her. Maybe he could convince her to stay with him, in his room until the warm weather came. He didn't think so, but maybe.

Why the school, though? She had people she could stay with, didn't she? No. People to use her, maybe, but not to take her in. But isn't that what she's doing to you? *She needs someone.* Exactly. She had nowhere else to turn. *Shut up. Just shut up.*

Ahead, the school came into view, closed only two years but falling to pieces. Had been, even back then.

The chain that secured the outer gymnasium entrance had been cut, and the door stood open. Stephen went inside. His footsteps echoed as he walked through the vast dark space toward the ground-level hallway, and as he was about to cross the threshold into the school's main corridor, a skittering sound startled him. He turned quickly, but it was just a bunch of dead leaves blowing across the floor.

#

At first she thought it was just animals—raccoons, maybe mice—but then she heard him call her name.

"Missy?" he whispered, even though there was no one else around to hear him.

"Over here," she said.

She had moved one of the cots from the nurse's office and had a small fire going in a metal wastebasket. Although the windows in the old Home Economics room were still intact, there were enough broken ones throughout the rest of the building to vent the smoke.

"You've seriously been stayin' here," he said.

"It's not so bad." She pulled a blanket, which she'd also found in the nurse's office, tighter around herself.

"I brought you some extra clothes and stuff," he said, unrolling the sleeping bag and setting the thermals and flannels on the end of the cot. He draped the sleeping bag over her legs. "This thing's good in subzero temps—had to save up for it."

"Thanks for coming," she said.

"You knew I would."

Of course she'd known.

She leaned over and placed a piece of splintered wood in the wastebasket—part of a cabinet, busted up by vandals—and the flame guttered. She watched the shadows on Stephen's face as he rifled through his backpack, removing cans and small cartons of food. She sometimes wondered why he had never tried anything with her like all the others. She knew he'd been kicked out of school several times for fighting, standing up for her when people began spreading rumors—some true, some not. Perhaps if she had let herself be with him, she wouldn't be in this situation. And why hadn't she ever wanted to be with him? It was a question she couldn't answer in any way that made sense to her. She wanted to hug him now, let him hold her, but she didn't want him to know, to feel what was under her clothes. It had been moving a lot more lately. But that was good. Movement was good.

It would be here any day now, she knew, and she told herself she wasn't worried. Everything would be fine.

He held up the lunch meat. "Are you hungry?"

When was the last time she had eaten? That morning: peanut butter sandwich and cold coffee, instant, taken from home. But that seemed like ages ago, and she was ravenous. Eating for two means you need to eat more. She had to remind herself of this often.

"A little," she said.

He passed her the package of bologna and a sleeve of saltines.

She tried not to eat too quickly, to show how hungry she really was, but the greasy, salty taste was the best thing she'd tasted in her whole life ever.

He opened a can of beef stew and, after looking around for a minute, went to one of the ovens along the wall. He removed a rack and placed it across the top of the wastebasket, then set the can of stew on it. The fire licked the bottom of the can and the label turned black.

He turned toward her. "Why are you doing this? It's crazy."

He looked concerned, a little desperate, even. Like he wanted to fix things but knew he couldn't. And that was true, she thought, he couldn't. No one could.

"I have my reasons," she said. "That's all I can say right now."

"Don't you trust me?"

"You know I trust you. But there's just some things people have to work through themselves." As she heard herself speak the words, she wondered if it was true.

It is. No, it isn't.

"You can stay with me," Stephen said. "You'll freeze to death if you stay here."

"I told you, it's not that bad." She put on a smile, hoping to convince him. "I'm fine. Look, I even got a bed."

She didn't like the way he rolled his eyes at her. If only she could tell him, he wouldn't be like this. No, he'd be even *more* insistent. She would tell him, she would, but not now, not until . . .

There were no spoons, but he located some bowls in a dusty cupboard, wiped them out with his shirt, and emptied half of the stew into each. Steam rose from the bowls as they sat there drinking the hot food, the only sounds coming from the crackling fire and their own breathing.

Stephen reached into the bag again and removed the jar of bourbon. He unscrewed the lid, held it up to his nose for a moment, and offered it to Missy. She shook her head. After taking a small sip himself, he replaced the lid and put it back, then offered her a cigarette from a flattened pack of Winstons. Again she shook her head. Several more moments of silence passed between them before Stephen said, "I sure wish you'd talk to me."

"I have been talking to you."

He looked frustrated. "You know what I mean."

"I'm sorry," she said. And she was sorry, so sorry in so many ways. But sorry doesn't change things, she knew that. She wished it did, but it didn't.

"If you won't stay with me, I'll stay here."

"No," she said.

"But what if someone comes? People break in here all the time."

"Not in the winter."

"You don't know that." His desperation had spread from his eyes to his voice.

"I can take care of myself," she told him.

"I wonder if you can."

She could tell by his face that he regretted saying it.

"I'll come back tomorrow at least," he said, and stood up, seeming resigned for the time being. "I'll see if I can get

179

some more food, too. This stuff should last you for a little while at least."

She, too, felt regret, for causing him to look so defeated. She smiled at him again in the flickering light of the fire. "Okay," she said. "I'd like that."

He went to leave, and she called, "Stephen, wait."

He turned to look at her.

"Promise you won't tell anyone," she said.

He was quiet.

"Please. Promise me."

He looked away. "I promise," he said, and a moment later he left.

She listened as his steps grew faint in the hall and then disappeared. Removing the oven rack from the wastebasket, she added some more debris to the fire. Then she curled up under the sleeping bag and blankets and closed her eyes. As she began to drift off, a plane passed faintly somewhere far above her.

#

He came back the next day like he said he would, in the morning, then again later. He brought her more food and some jugs of water. "Have to stay hydrated," he told her. But then the storm came in the middle of the night, its wind rattling the glass in the remaining windows, whistling through the broken ones, blowing dirt and leaves and loose papers down the dark hallways, and he didn't come back again. Must have been snowed in, she told herself.

She had no sense of time after that.

It was cold, but *she* wasn't that cold. Always kept a small fire going. Plenty of things to burn—broken furniture and books. She hated to burn the books because books are how you learn but learning to survive sometimes meant burning things. Even books. She burned as few as possible at first, but the lighter fluid she'd bought at Mort's ran out and she needed the paper.

The sleeping bag Stephen had brought her helped, too. Good in subzero temps, he'd said. Then he'd called you crazy. *But he didn't really mean crazy. Did he? Of course not.* But you have to be to be here. You have to be crazy.

The contractions had come and gone for months. Just the body preparing itself, that's all. Called Braxton Hicks after the doctor who first studied them, that's what the books she'd checked out from the Middleton library had said. Different from the real thing. Walking helped ease the discomfort, so with the extra layers of clothes and the sleeping bag wrapped around her, she walked the perimeter of the room, the length of the hallway, but tried to stay close, always close to the bed and the fire, always avoiding windows because of wind and eyes.

But during the storm, there had been no eyes, definitely no eyes, barely any windows for eyes to see through. Just the howling white.

Then, days after—how many?—the warm wetness, the real contractions. Not Braxton Hicks this time. The real thing. Showtime, she thought, and did all the things the books had told her to do: changed positions often, rested, focused on her breathing, moved around—moving can be soothing, like the wind, helps speed things along.

For the first time since finding out, since she had first understood what was happening to her, she was really afraid. Thirty-seven weeks, more or less, and now the fear. So much fear.

The contractions were getting worse, more painful. That's how she knew they were the real thing this time. The vise around her middle. The body tensing, the wincing. But warm, surprisingly warm. Fingers and toes stinging a little, but not too bad. Tightening. Almost steals the breath right from you but no, not too cold. Adrenaline keeps you warm, or makes you feel warm. Hypothermia: stop being cold just fall asleep. *No, I won't do that, I won't.*

Another—tighter this time. Crushing.

"Water," she said in a low, dry voice. Have to stay hydrated. He'd said that. And the books had said so because water eased pain.

She found one of the small jugs—frozen.

"Oh no," she said, and her eyes began to tear up. After a moment, she said it again: "Oh no." But this time she wiped her tears. This was your choice.

What choice? There was no choice. Never a choice. They'd take it away. It didn't matter if she did it all on her own.

"They'll take it away," she muttered as she used the knife she'd brought for protection to cut open the plastic jug. She chipped off a large chunk of ice, placed it in an empty soup can, and set it over the fire.

Tightening. Crushing. Change position, breathe.

When the ice melted, she drank it. Warm and soothing.

"They'll take it away."

Don't even know what it is. Doesn't even have a name.

"It's mine," she said, and sipped the water.

When the can was empty, the fear moved back in her mind, and her heart took over. *I can do this on my own, I can bring it into this world. I can take it away before they do. I can go somewhere, anywhere, I can—*

Tightening. Crushing.

"Lie back," she told herself. "Breathe. Just breathe." It's natural, she thought, this pain. Oxytocin causes contractions. The books all said so.

They won't take it. I'll take it before they can. "Trust me," she whispered to the life inside her, the small life clinging to her, being squeezed, being forced out. "They won't take you from me, I promise." But deep in the center of her chest, she felt it was a promise she couldn't keep.

Tightening. Crushing.

"I love you," she whispered.

She prepared herself. She stoked the flames in the wastebasket until she could feel the heat on her face and then peeled down the wet long johns under her skirt. She rested on the bed, her own backpack, which she'd filled with random provisions before leaving the house for the last time, under her for support. She pulled the blanket and sleeping bag over her body again, just before another crushing contraction.

Lie back. Breathe.

It's coming.

#

The power went out for an entire day, and when it finally came back on, the phones were still down.

Missy had seemed okay when he went to see her the day before the storm, took her more soup, meat, and bread. And water. It's the most important thing, he'd told her. You can get by for a long time with just water.

She'd insisted she was warm enough, but he'd brought her another blanket, too. He was glad he'd done that. She was so damn stubborn about things, he'd always known that about her, but this was ridiculous. Insane is what it was. Who camped out in the winter when they didn't have to? Homeless people and people on the run, that's who. He supposed they were all running to or from one thing or another. But why not at least wait until summer?

School was cancelled for two days, and as soon as the storm was over, his old man put him to work. No lazing when there's money to be made. It had snowed so much they couldn't get out the front door of the house—drift clear up to the top of the jamb—so he had to use the side door. "Go around and shovel a path," his father said. "Spread some salt. Then get your ass out there and do some driveways."

Stephen worked his way through the trailer park near their house. Five bucks each. Money to put toward the electric bill, the phone, the old man's case a day of PBR.

He thought about Missy, told himself she was fine. She was stubborn but strong, had to be to put up with all the talk. If only she'd tell him what it was. More than just a fight with her mother, of that he was certain. But she would be okay.

Except he couldn't know that, could he? She was protected from the worst of the cold, sure, maybe even more than some folks. The room she was in still had all its windows. And she had a fire, was smart enough to drag a cot in so she wasn't on the floor. Hell, she might have even gone home before it got really bad.

Each afternoon, Stephen's old man took the money he'd made shoveling, stuffed it in his pocket without a word, and ordered him to bring in more wood. Take out the trash. Cook up some supper. Since the power had been restored, his father hardly seemed to move from his spot in front of the TV. Not once did he leave the house, having stocked up before the storm: a few cases and plenty of smokes. And there was always the Wild Turkey in the cupboard, which he'd start in on when the beer ran low.

You should just go and see her, he kept telling himself. Let the old bastard do his own shoveling. But he didn't go, didn't want to deal with his father, to face the inevitable rage that would erupt if he didn't do what he was told. Did that make him a coward? The more he thought about it, the more he thought it probably did.

It was Sunday evening when he finally decided to do something. He couldn't just let her stay there, couldn't just let her act this way and not try to do something about it.

But you promised, and that's supposed mean something even if nothing else does.

"Maybe it does," he said to himself as he lay on his bed staring at the dirty cobwebs collected in the corners of the ceiling. "But to hell with that."

She has food and water and heat. People have survived worse.

But I'd never forgive myself.

He walked to the kitchen, which separated the hallway and the living room, where his father sat in his filthy chair. The phone had come back on earlier that morning, so he lifted the receiver from its cradle on the wall and dialed zero for the operator. He'd heard somewhere that 911 put you through to the city or the county and was for emergencies

186

only. This was an emergency, wasn't it? He wasn't sure. Best to call direct.

He stretched the coiled cord to the end of the hallway where his old man wouldn't hear. Probably passed out anyway. But just then he heard his father move in the other room, make a hacking noise, and go quiet again. Still awake, but not for long.

"Lornfield police department," he whispered into the mouthpiece.

The phone rang on the other end, and when someone picked up, Stephen was silent for a long time. Second thoughts. You promised.

"Hello?" the voice said again. "This is the police department. Hello? Who is this?"

Don't give your name.

"I wanna report someone . . . in the old school."

Idiot.

"Missy . . . Missy Foster."

"Who's calling? Speak up, please."

Hang up.

He hung up.

Betrayal. That's what they called it. Broken promises. But maybe saved lives. Sure, you keep telling yourself that.

He thought about going to her now, asking for forgiveness beforehand, but he wouldn't make it in time, not on foot, and not in this weather. Still too bad out. Too far. Besides, the cops would be on their way, wouldn't they? He hoped so and he hoped not. She wouldn't even know it was him who told. Yes, she would. No one else knows she's there. Just you. And you promised.

#

Late July, and she again stood outside Stephen's bedroom window, tapping on the glass. After a minute had passed, he lifted the blinds. The look on his face was one of stunned surprise, but then it resolved into a smile. He simply stared at her at first, standing in the balmy night wearing a tight Led Zeppelin T-shirt and jeans tucked into her well-worn combat boots. Her hair was cut shorter than when he'd last seen her, styled in a way that seemed to accentuate the soft curve of her jaw.

"Missy," he said, "where you been? I came by your house, but your mom said you went to stay with an aunt or something."

"Can you come out?"

"Yeah, give me a sec."

She watched as he peeked out his bedroom door, probably to see what his dad was doing. He always had to tip-toe around, she remembered, especially when his father was drinking. She'd had to sneak out herself, just to come see him. "I don't think you should go anywhere for a while," her

188

mom had said. "Not so soon after coming home." She was trying, though, her mom. She'd really stepped up. More than Missy ever would have thought.

"So you were at your aunt's, huh?" Stephen asked after he climbed out the window.

She didn't want to tell him the truth, not yet: that she'd been in Southwood Pines for the last six months. And everything else—those last nights in the school, the baby. Part of her knew that he wouldn't think less of her, not Stephen. But still. He didn't need to know just now, maybe not at all, after so much time.

"Yeah, up by Cleveland," she said. "I finished junior year up there, but I'm gonna have to do summer school to make up for some classes I flunked."

"Bummer," he said.

"Yeah."

"When'd you get back?"

"Yesterday," she said. "I was gonna call you while I was gone, but my aunt's a nut about long distance." She felt guilty about how easily the lie had poured out of her.

"That's okay." He shrugged. "You're here now."

She grinned at him and sat down cross-legged against the side of the house.

He sat down next to her, his knees bent, bare feet in the dead grass. "So, how long did you camp out in the school before you went home?"

"Not long," she said. "About a day after the last time you came."

He looked troubled. "I tried to come back," he said, "but the storm . . . When I finally made it, you weren't there anymore." This was the truth. He had gone back, the day after making the call to the cops. Stephen thought now that at least she didn't know he had called them. Not if she'd left beforehand like she said.

"I understand," she assured him. "I wouldn't have wanted you to come when it was so bad out, anyway." Missy knew it was him who had called the police. She hadn't known right away, of course, not with so much happening in her body and her mind and her heart, but she'd put it together in time. He was the only one it could have been. She didn't resent him for it, though. Things had worked out. Still, she wondered if the lie was eating him up inside. Like hers was beginning to.

"Was it your mom?" he asked. "Who made you leave and go to your aunt's, I mean?"

"We both agreed it was best for a while, and things are better now. She even cut back on her drinkin'." Missy laughed. "We've actually been gettin' along for once. It's like some kind of miracle."

Stephen nodded. He thought about telling her how nothing had changed with the old man—still a bastard—but he didn't want to get into that. Not now, not when it was such a nice night with the stars and smell of grass and her warm body beside him.

"Summer school," he said. "That's pretty lame."

"It's better than not graduating on time, I guess," she said.

"Another year. It'll finally be over after that. Then it's . . ." He trailed off, not knowing how to finish.

No, not over, she thought. *It'll be just the beginning.* Her mother, much to Missy's surprise, had refused to let her give up the baby, even after the social worker insisted it would be wisest. "No grandchild of mine's gettin' put in the system," she'd said. Missy was amazed at this, and that they'd even given them the choice. The baby had been under weight when they'd brought the two of them in, luckily not fatally so. She shuddered and felt tears threaten to spill over when she remembered those nights in the darkness, the cold. And she would always remember. The translucent cord, still attached, the way she saw for the first time, in the light of the ambulance, just before the sedative drove her eyelids down, her son's tiny body, so fragile, still covered in a waxy layer of vernix—that's what the books had called it, vernix, protects the baby's skin. He had nursed—that's what saved him, they'd said. But neither of them would have survived much longer, not in the cold. She was thankful for Stephen, that he had broken his promise. He'd saved them both.

191

She wanted to tell him everything. And she assured herself that she would. Soon.

She thought about her son, whom she had named Dustin because she thought it was a nice name, strong, and it had come to her like a kind of light. Dustin would never know his father, nor would she. There had been at least three of them. And when the day came that he finally asked, *Where's my daddy?* what would she tell him? In time, maybe she'd have an answer.

Stephen would be a good father, she thought, but she could never expect something like that from him, it wouldn't be right. She believed he would accept the responsibility, but it wasn't his.

She leaned against him and they sat in silence. Some time passed and a dog barked somewhere. Then another. He wanted to tell her that he was sorry he had betrayed her, but instead he just rested his head against hers and listened.

"You can kiss me if you want," she said.

He could feel the vibration of the words travel from her and into him and through his entire body. It was all he'd wanted for the longest time, ever since they were young, even when they were little and left alone while their parents went out drinking. Always just friends, though. Which was okay, because it would change things between them.

She wanted to tell him she loved him, maybe always had loved him, but she waited to see if he would do it, what he'd never done.

I love you, he thought. *Yes, it's definitely love.* Then he said, "Maybe later," and grasped her hand. He squeezed it gently. "Let's just sit a while."

The Sailor and the Saint

At the bottom of the stairs, the smell of burning bacon and stale tobacco smoke hits me like a smack to the face. Except for a little movement in the other room, the house is quiet. The living room is dim, the only light a dull gray ribbon of morning leaking through the vertical break between the curtains. I take in the scene: the broken lamp on the end table, how the couch and chair are shifted a little from their usual positions, a reminder that the virtual silence is a deception. Just one of many calms, following and preceding one of many storms I've grown to anticipate.

Although he's been dead for years, my grandfather speaks, as if behind me, just over my shoulder. *You can't change the wind.* It's something he used to say to me when I was little, something I never understood but that always seems to come back to me whenever I feel trapped. It wasn't until the other morning, when I remembered the second half of the saying, that I finally got what he meant by it. I woke up out of a dead sleep and it floated there in the dark like a residual image: *But you can adjust your sails.* Hours later, as night and day began to merge outside my window, it was still there, as if demanding to be acknowledged, and I wondered how I could have forgotten it.

Out in the kitchen, things appear back to normal. Frank sits looking like a sullen donkey, drinking coffee and chain smoking at the table. He's in his boxers and a worn-out sleeveless T-shirt with a picture of a hotrod on it. When I walk into the room, he peers at me through the thick cloud of cigarette smoke that swirls between us. "Shouldn't you be out looking for a job or something?" he says, lighting a fresh cigarette off the butt of the old one and blowing the smoke in my direction. I could ask him the same question.

When Frank hooked up with Mom, just after Grandpa died, he had big plans to open his own business, one that sold "pre-owned" furniture and appliances. But the bank wouldn't give him the loan because his credit was shit. Since then he's made a steady career out of being a leech, drinking and gambling up Mom's money while she busts her ass cleaning motel rooms for just over minimum wage.

"It's only eight o'clock," I say, not bothering to wave the smoke away. "Most places worth applying to won't even be open till nine."

He lets out something between a grunt and a snort before taking another drag off his Camel. "You better get moving, just the same, because I've been talking to your mother, and I think it's about time you start paying some rent around here."

I had always planned on moving out by the time I turned eighteen, but things don't always work out, and I'm about two years late on the follow through. Up until last week, I'd been working part-time as a line cook at this little dive across the river, doing my best to lighten Mom's financial burden by not asking her for anything but a bed to sleep in. But one night the owner's lush of a wife got bitter when I didn't return her advances, told him I grabbed her ass in the walk-in cooler. Although I thought I saw doubt in his eyes when he confronted me about it, in the end, it was her word against mine. And that was that. Yesterday, when I went to pick up my last paycheck, I slashed the tires of his Town Car and pissed in his gas tank, thinking I would feel vindicated. But all it did was make me feel guilty, because I was going to quit that lousy job anyway.

"I've got some places in mind to go," I say to Frank. "So I'll be out of the way and you can continue doing . . . whatever the hell it is you do around here all damn day."

He glares at me. "Watch it," he says.

Mom says, "Make sure you eat something before you leave, Jimmy." She's been multitasking her way between the stove and the hallway mirror, applying her makeup and fixing her hair.

"I'm not really hungry," I say, zipping up my hoodie and leaning against the counter.

"Well, at least take a piece of fruit with you. You're skinny as a rail."

I grab an apple from the fruit bowl beside the microwave and tuck it into the pocket of my sweatshirt as she continues her run back and forth, flipping eggs and bacon in the skillet while she gets ready.

Frank finishes his coffee and holds out his empty cup for a refill. I just stare in amazement, my eyes moving from his cup to his face. Finally I say, "You know, she's not your goddamn waitress, man."

He glances up at me, a look of surprise on his face. Usually I avoid making waves with Frank, even small ones. I've learned that defiance and contention only cause problems, for me and her. Once, when he and Mom had been together for only a few months, I'd rolled my eyes at him when he was drunk. He grabbed me by the throat with a quickness I wasn't expecting. "Gonna have to teach you some manners," he said, grinning as he spoke. When Mom came to my defense, he snapped at her. "Dammit, Laura, kid's got no fuckin' respect!" She was as shocked as I was at his outburst, and how afterward he snatched his keys off the hook by the back door and stormed outside, spitting gravel against the side of the house as he peeled out of the driveway. He came back the next day, saying he was sorry and clutching a pitiful bouquet of flowers he'd probably picked up at the gas station. But I could tell from the look in his eyes the night before: we'd finally met the real Frank.

That was about three years ago. And ever since it's as if we've been tiptoeing through a mine field, just waiting to take one wrong step.

"I said watch it, boy," he says. "I won't repeat myself a third time. Get your ass gone before you say something you regret."

Mom's rushing around so frantically that she hasn't acknowledged mine and Frank's little interaction. Either that

198

or she's been pretending not to. But with his last remark, she seems to tense up a little, like she's bracing herself.

But I don't bother responding to Frank's threat. Don't bother to say, Oh I'll be going, all right. For her, I decide to leave it alone. I just think, *Soon enough, you prick,* and head for the door.

Then I stop, mid-stride. I recall once hearing someone say you should never part with people you care about when you're in a bad mood, because you never know if that's the last time you'll see them. But I do know. And although I don't give a damn about Frank, I don't want my last memory of this morning to be his miserable face.

"I love you, Mom," I say.

It's enough to stop her in her tracks. I don't know the last time I said those words to her, but the fact that I can't remember means it's been too long. I turn around and cross the kitchen, standing in her path between the stove and the hallway. She pauses in the middle of tying her hair back, looks up at me. She grins, but there's uncertainty in it, as if she's not quite sure she heard me correctly.

So I hug her.

"Well, I love you too, sweetheart," she says, and when I pull away after a moment, the confused quality of her expression has softened. She looks less doubtful now as the corners of her mouth break into a smile.

Behind her, Frank's usual sneer of contempt deepens into a hateful scowl as he gets up from the table and pours himself some more coffee.

Mom and I part, and I hurry back across the room, stepping out on the back stoop and shutting the door behind me before Frank can say anything else.

The image of Mom smiling as she does her hair—that's the last thing I want to remember.

#

I considered taking off many times when I was younger, but thinking about it was as far as I ever got. I'd often lie awake at night, going through my options—joining the circus, roadie for a rock band, maybe—but after the absurdity of such possibilities brought me back to reality, the conclusion was always the same: I had no place to go. Things haven't changed as far as that goes, but the absence of refuge is no longer enough to keep me from getting out.

Earlier this morning I stuffed the last of what I'll be taking with me into my grandfather's military duffel, which had been stored in an old chest in the corner of the basement for the last fifty years of his life. He died a few summers ago. Mom and I had been living with him since I was about fourteen, just after my dad blew his brains out with a shotgun in the garage of our old house. No one knew why he did it. He left a note on his workbench that just said, *It's better this way.* That's it. And I'm still trying to find the truth in those four words.

Grandpa's place is where Mom had grown up until she was seventeen and decided to tune in and drop out and caught the whole barefoot-freewheeling-toward-San Francisco bug that everyone else was catching back then. Back when things were cheaper and safer and people still believed they could change the world with flowers and hugs. It was ten years before she came back to Ohio and met my dad, another three before she had me. But even though we lived in the same small city, we hardly ever saw my grandfather except on Christmas. When we moved in, it was obvious that, despite the unfortunate circumstances, the old man liked having us around as he neared the finish line himself.

Mom and I were the only family he had left when his liver finally went out on him, and although he didn't own much—just the house, a few weathered antiques, and some mementos from his time in the service—he'd left it all to us in his will. When the lawyer read through the short document, he stated that Grandpa specifically wanted "my only ever grandson" to have his military duffel bag, though I couldn't figure at the time why it was so important to him that I have it. We'd never been particularly close over the years, having spent so little time together. But when we did visit, and more so after we started living in his house, I'd often sit with him while he took long pulls from a pint of Jim Beam and recounted his days in the war—*Stickin' it to them damn krauts*, he was fond of saying. I suppose I felt connected to him in a way I'd never felt connected to anyone. So when his old saying about the wind and the sails came back to me the other day, like a whisper carried on a current of air, I couldn't help thinking maybe the duffel had been some sort of sign that I'd been just too blind to see.

I packed light: a few pairs of clothes, my portable CD player and a small booklet of CDs, a flashlight, extra batteries, and a buck knife I found among some other bric-a-brac in the basement when we were sorting through Grandpa's things.

Before I went downstairs, I looked around my room to see if there was anything else that I couldn't do without, but there was nothing else I could think of, other than maybe a little food and the money I've been socking away since my birthday. I turned twenty about two months back, just after St. Patrick's Day, and though I never ask Mom for a single cent if I can help it, she slipped a card with twenty bucks in it into my coat pocket when I wasn't looking. Inside the card, written in her loopy script, was an apology—*Sorry it couldn't be more*—and her trademark heart with an arrow through it. She told me to go out and treat myself to something, but I tucked it away. When I got my next paycheck, I tucked half of that away, too. And when I cash the check that's in my pocket, I'll have just over three-hundred fifty bucks to get me going. I'd feel better if it was more, of course, but I'll just have to make do. If all goes well, I'll end up somewhere where I can find a job washing cars or bussing tables or mopping floors. Honestly, living here as long as I have, I've learned to aim low in matters of vocation.

When I was done packing, I dropped the duffel bag out my window, where it landed with a flat thump beside the front porch. I was about to head downstairs when I remembered something and walked back to the crude bookshelf I'd fashioned out of cinderblocks and pieces of old lumber from behind the garage. I pulled out a small photo album that was wedged between a large dictionary and an anthology of Modernist poetry and prose that my high school English teacher gave me in an admirable attempt to nurture my creativity and future scholarly endeavors. He was a great teacher, and I didn't have the heart to tell him how I really felt about James Joyce and many of his contemporaries.

Flipping through the album, page after page of awkward pictures of me from various stages of my childhood, I soon found what I was looking for: a picture of me and Mom on the shore of Lake Michigan. I'm about twelve in the photo, my messy hair hanging in my eyes, while Mom's auburn hair dances in the breeze coming off the water. She stands with her arm around my shoulders, wearing a pair of big sunglasses that makes her look like a movie star. The picture was taken at some summer arts festival in Milwaukee, where we'd gone to visit one of Mom's old girlfriends. They'd spent that week smoking weed and playing records, trying to relive their long lost hippiedom. I enjoyed it, seeing her like that.

I peeled back the thin plastic that held it in place and removed the photograph, setting the album back on the shelf. Just before sticking the picture in my wallet, I thought that the people in the picture almost looked like strangers, and it took me a moment to realize it was because we were both smiling.

#

The morning is overcast, and there's an electric quality to the air, a smell of ozone that hints at rain. After removing a piece of broken trellis, I stash the duffel under the front porch and walk to the end of our street. As I look down the hill to my right, the shabby houses and abandoned mills across the freeway sit like fading memories beneath a washed-out sky, and I find it hard to believe that things were ever better than they are now, that the city hasn't always been so hopeless. Before my time.

On the corner up ahead is the Hilltop Tavern, one of those places that opens at 6 a.m. and caters to former steelworkers and other old-timers, who spend their days pining over the lives they used to live before the world went to hell. Inside, a few men sit in the gloom as I pass. The faint sound of a talk-radio show comes out through the open front door, and the neon Pabst Blue Ribbon sign in the window seems like the only spot of color in the gray morning.

Hanging a left at the Hilltop, I start walking toward the West Side. I've got a couple stops to make today before leaving, and since they're on different sides of town, it could take a while, so I stick out my thumb.

I'm not a seasoned hitchhiker, so I've been practicing every day for the last few weeks, just bumming rides from strangers from one place to another, down the street, across town, wherever. Just trying to get a feel for it.

After being denied a few times, an old clunker of a Cadillac slows to a stop. The car's windows are down, and a middle-aged black man leans over to talk to me through the passenger side. He's wearing a Cleveland Browns cap, and the top few buttons of his loose-fitting Hawaiian shirt are undone, revealing a gold cross on a chain around his neck.

"Where you headin,' young blood?"

"West Side," I say. "Calvary Cemetery, you know where that is?"

"Yeah, I know where it's at. Not too far out my way, neither. Hop on in."

As the car sputters its way toward another rise in the landscape, which will eventually level off for a bit before becoming a series of smaller hills and valleys, the thought of taking off and leaving Mom alone with that asshole Frank suddenly makes my heart tighten, like it's being squeezed in a giant fist. But that's exactly what I'm going to do. Say some goodbyes, retrieve my things from beneath the porch, then gone. I assure myself that the pangs of remorse and sadness will make way for new, more pleasant feelings eventually.

And even if the image of her in the kitchen this morning, smiling as she did her hair, slowly disappears from my mind as the miles between us grow, I tell myself I still have the photograph of us on the lakefront to remind me. We were happy once.

#

Calvary Cemetery is located on a stretch of road that cuts a ragged path through the West Side toward downtown, sandwiched between a tattoo shop and a liquor store. When

I come here, which hasn't been often lately, I imagine people burying their dead, memorializing them in ink, then stopping in for a bottle to kick off the grieving process, as if this particular section of street is a sort of grim strip mall.

As I pass through the gate, following the winding asphalt, the smell of the impending thunderstorm becomes infused with the sweet smell of hyacinth, lilac, and various other flowers which decorate many of the graves. Several hundred yards in front of me, marking the innermost section of the cemetery, is a sight almost farcical: towering above headstones of different shapes and sizes is a large stone crucifix, its surface pink and displaying a lurid painting of Christ in all his emaciated glory. The image, among all the other stones and their sullen, muted grays, is almost enough to make my head hurt.

Beyond the concrete monstrosity, near a chain-link fence bordering the back edge of the property, is my grandfather's grave, a simple, unassuming slab of granite in the shade of budding elm tree. He rests beside his wife, a grandmother I never knew because she passed before I was born. Although my relationship with the old man was in its infancy when he died, I felt compelled to come here, to pay my respects one last time.

With no one besides my mom and me to tend to it, the plot has become overgrown. We both kept up on it for a while, visiting a couple times a month to replace the shriveled flowers and to let him know we miss him and all that. But time has a way of leading people to distraction, I suppose. After a while, the currents of life sort of just drag them away from the few things that really matter and toward whatever keeps them getting by in the world.

I kneel down and begin to tear out grass by the fistful.

"Hey, old man," I say, brushing away the dirt that's collected in the grooves of his name. I don't really know what to say and feel kind of goofy. It's a strange thing, talking to the dead like you talk to the living. But I've come clear across town, so I do my best. "I'm leaving tonight," I say, "and just thought I should drop by, you know, to say I still think about you and wish I'd have come by more often."

A fire truck screams down the street, and a few moments later an ambulance wails in its wake, lights flashing, horn blaring as it speeds toward some urban catastrophe.

"Anyway," I continue, "I'm finally gonna put that duffel bag of yours to some use." I'm stalling, making small talk, not saying what I need to say. So I let out a heavy sigh and start over. "You were a good man, the only person who ever gave a damn about us, especially after Dad went and checked out, and I'm sorry if it seems like we forgot about you. It's just, Mom's with this joker Frank now. Mean bastard. Started seeing him right after you died. He takes up every minute of her time when she's not working to support his lazy ass." I pick up a small pile of dirt, let it run through my fingers. "But we haven't forgotten you," I say. "At least I haven't. I've been thinking about that thing you always used to say to me, how you can't control the wind, but you can adjust the sails?" I realize that I've phrased it as a question, as if waiting for him to acknowledge me. "I never really knew what it meant back when you were alive, and now I'm wondering if maybe the reason you never explained it to me was because you wanted me to think on it and figure it out on my own."

Again I pause, this time wishing for some sort confirmation but knowing it won't come.

"I've decided I'm leaving. I can't stay in that house anymore. This city. It's like I'm suffocating. I feel bad just splitting, but it's all I can think to do. Frank and I don't exactly see eye to eye, and it seems like maybe Mom'll be better off if I'm not around."

There's no logical reason for me to think this, of course. In fact, hadn't Dad made the exact same assumption before pulling the trigger? Maybe I'm no better. Maybe I'm taking the easy way out.

So be it, then.

I spend a little while longer talking, stuttering off and on as I vent about life at home and justifying my decision. But eventually I just find myself talking in circles, saying I can't stay, and I feel bad but I'm leaving anyway and that's that, and on and on, as if hoping he'll speak up and say, *Look, Jimmy Boy, you do what you gotta do. You adjust your sails and go wherever they take you.*

But despite hearing the old man's voice as recently as this morning, I'm discovering a cold truth: the dead don't talk—at least, not when you want them to.

"So that's about it," I say, pressing my hand to the cool stone. "Maybe I'll see you on the other side someday, sooner or later." Then I rise to my feet and follow the winding path back the way I came, past the garish monument of God's only son, past the bundles of cloying blossoms tucked in their vases, and back out into the land of the living where hopefully I can catch a ride.

#

When I leave the cemetery, I stop into the liquor store to cash my paycheck. Most stores around here will cash checks for a charge of about ten percent, give or take. It's not exactly legal, but they get away with it because for people without bank accounts, it's often the only option.

A few minutes later I get picked up by a thin-faced man with stringy blond hair named Dwight. His White Zombie T-shirt is holey and sun-faded, and he's got silver skull rings on both hands. He keeps drumming on the dashboard of his pickup truck as he jabbers at me over the stereo about whores and stripping copper from vacant houses for beer money. He tells me he's from some little Podunk town called Miles Junction about a half hour outside the city, but I can't seem to get much else out of him in the way of conversation. Nor do I really care to.

He pulls out a bottle of Mad Dog from under the seat and offers it to me. But I get a good look at his yellow teeth and dry, cracked lips, and say, "I'm good."

He shrugs. "More for me," he says, unscrewing the cap and taking a swig. Then he tucks it back under the seat and

209

resumes banging on the dash with his rings. "Fuckin' copper, brother!" he yells, swerving erratically to avoid a pothole. "Fuckin' whores!"

I need to get out of this truck. Luckily, we're close to my stop. Isabelle's is only a few blocks from here and I'd rather walk the rest of the way.

"Right up here's good," I tell him, pointing to the drive-thru on the corner.

"You got it," he says, and cuts into the parking lot without slowing down. He slams on the breaks and the truck jerks to a halt beside a busted payphone.

"Thanks for the lift," I say, trying not to look too unnerved as I get out.

He tells me, "Take 'er sleazy, brother." Then something down the street seems to catch his attention, something perhaps that's not really there, and he screeches out of the parking lot without another word, barely missing a minivan coming through the intersection.

#

Isabelle's a girl from the East Side that I run around with from time to time. "Friends with benefits" she calls us. We met one weekend when my buddy Nick and I bused it out to the burbs to dick around at the mall for a few hours. Isabelle and a couple of her girlfriends were in the food court. She was eating a slice of pizza and drinking an Orange Julius. I had never been very bold, but she looked right at me as we walked by, and for some reason I worked up the nerve to ask for her number. We hooked up the following weekend, and it sort of became a regular thing, though I suspect the only reason she continues to mess around with me is because of her parents. They despise me, and I think she gets a thrill out of it. They're Puerto Rican, and the idea of their beautiful daughter—their *only* daughter—hooking up with some white trash from the South Side apparently leaves a bad taste in their mouths.

I can't say I blame them. After all, I have no illusions about being "a keeper" or whatever. There's nothing driving me forward in life other than a nagging call from everywhere but here. Frankly, I know as well as they do that she can do much better. Isabelle has no illusions either. We turn each other on and get each other off. We smoke a little weed. Sometimes we talk about things. But we've always understood what our relationship is. Not that we don't care for each other; in whatever way two horny young people can bring themselves to care for each other, I imagine we do, and maybe even a little more. But neither of us ever saw it as something that would last.

When I talked to her last night, I told her I needed to see her, and she said she'd be home this afternoon because she was suspended from school for ten days. Isabelle's eighteen and finishing up her senior year. But apparently she got into it with some black girl who'd called her a spic in the cafeteria earlier this week, and now the principal says she can't attend the graduation ceremony. According to her, she "ripped that bitch's weave right the fuck out." That made me laugh when she told me, picturing her all revved up and scrapping like one of the guys.

She answers the door wearing purple pajama bottoms and a spaghetti-strap top with lace around the hem and neckline. Her thick brown hair is tied back into a high ponytail and her dark skin makes me think of summertime and hot, sandy beaches.

"Hey," she says, smiling.

"Hey." I peer past her, searching for any sign of her parents.

"You coming in or what?" she says, putting one hand on her hip, running the fingertips of the other one along a strand of hair that's come loose. She assured me when we talked on the phone that her parents would be at work, and that we'd have the house to ourselves, but we've nearly been caught on several occasions, high as the sky and wrapped up in each other, so I'm a little paranoid. The last time I was here, I was in the middle of going down on her when we heard the door shut downstairs. And to make matters worse, Isabelle held me there, insisting that I finish before I snuck out. As pissed as I acted at the time, in retrospect I have to admit that it's just that kind of crazy stuff that makes life worth living.

"You sure your parents aren't gonna show up?" I ask, continuing to peek past her through the doorway, expecting her mom or dad to pop out from around a corner.

"Shit, they won't be home till way later."

212

"You've said that before."

"It's all good," she says. "Don't worry about it." Then her smile goes from pretty to full-on sexy as she grabs me by the strings of my hoodie and pulls me into the house, locking the door behind us.

#

"You could always come with me," I say.

We're lying naked in her bed, passing a joint back and forth, her hair a mess on the pillow. Some hip-hop artist I'm unfamiliar with raps over a drum machine on the stereo, which is turned down low enough for us to hear if anyone comes home.

"You're crazy," she says. "And do what? Sleep in a ditch, probably starve to death while waiting for some psycho trucker to give us a ride? Thanks, but I'll pass."

"Yeah, I figured. Just a thought."

She gets up and pulls on some snug boy-cut panties that hug her ass and make the under curves of her cheeks look like brown half-moons. I'll miss this thing we have, I tell myself, even if it doesn't really amount to more than being fuck buddies.

"Look, Jimmy," she says, turning to face me from across the room, "we both knew this"—she makes a gesture back and forth between us—"wasn't anything serious, just us having fun, so I ain't gonna give you no shit about leaving. And I ain't gonna try talking you into staying." She walks back toward me, her firm breasts moving with the cadence of her steps and snatches the joint from me as I'm about to take a hit. She tokes it, holds it, and exhales a long stream of smoke into the ceiling fan. "But I sure as fuck ain't gonna act grateful that you'd invite me along."

She's getting fired up, and I'm too stoned to argue. But for someone who claims to not care what I choose to do, she seems set on talking about it.

Lying here, hands behind my head, watching the fan circling in the center of the room above her, feeling its buffeting breeze, I say, "I don't expect you to act grateful. I don't expect anything. I just thought I'd bring it up. It's not like I thought you'd actually say yes."

The joint's almost gone, and she snuffs out the roach on the top of a Pepsi can on her dresser. Then she picks up a stuffed rabbit from her bookshelf and throws it at me. "So you were just playing games, then?"

I sit up and roll my eyes. "No, I wasn't playing games. That's not what I meant. Jesus Christ."

"Don't go talkin' at me with the Lord's name like that."

I forgot, this is one of those "never use the Lord's name in vain" households. I consider asking what the Almighty would think of our little pre-marital trysts, among other things. But that would just piss her off even more, and she might throw something harder at me next time.

"Sorry," I say. "Why are we even discussing it if we both agree that this"—I make the same back and forth gesture that she made—"was never anything more than what it is? Let's just drop it, can we?"

Standing with her feet rooted to the floor, smooth legs like tawny stone, she cocks her hip to the side, purses her lips, and crosses her arms over her bare chest. She just stares at me for a minute, then says, "Whatever," and turns her back to me, starts flipping through her CDs.

I secretly envy Isabelle. She has strong family ties. She has faith in things she can't see. To some, that might not seem like much, but to me it seems like winning the lottery.

"Hey," I say, "come here."

She ignores me. After a minute of silence, I get up and go to her, putting my arms around her from behind. She turns around and pushes me. It's playful enough, so I don't say anything. Then she pushes me again. And again. Each time I step back a little until she pushes me onto the bed. She straddles me and pins my arms with her knees.

Her smile is back.

We spend the rest of the day in bed—that is, when we're not doing it on her desk, or the floor. Or trying new things on the chair and, at one point, over the windowsill that looks out on her neighbor's yard, where someone's mowing the lawn. We stay stoned. We make each other feel good, knowing it will soon be over.

#

My first thought as I hear her father coming up the stairs calling, "Isabelle?" is *Shit, we fell asleep.*

I jump to my feet and scramble to gather up my clothes while she goes to the door to make sure it's locked. Then I kiss her hard on the mouth and head for the window just as her father starts knocking. "Isabelle? Are you in there?" He rattles the doorknob. "Isabelle?"

"Just a minute, Papi. I'm getting changed."

"Is there someone in there with you?"

"No, Papi . . . be right there."

I'm halfway out the window when she rushes over to her dresser and grabs something that's hanging from her lamp. She hurries over to me, loops a thin chain over my head, and when I glance down, a small medallion swings across my chest.

"Saint Christopher," she says. "He'll watch over you wherever you go."

Her father's pounding on the door now. *"Isabelle! Who's in there?!"*

I look into her dark eyes. She cradles my face in her hands, kisses me again. "If you decide to stay," she whispers, "hit me up. Now go."

We smile at each other one last time before she lowers the window blind. Then, as quickly as I can, I shimmy half-naked down a drain spout to where the rest of my things lay heaped in the driveway beside her father's car.

216

#

The rain came and went while we slept, and it's left the air damp and the street coated in a slick sheen. The clock on Isabelle's dresser read almost 9:00 when her father's voice woke us. It's now mostly dark out. What remains of the day is little more than a violet smear in the western sky. The street lamps have begun to flicker and hum, and the lights of downtown look like dying stars in the distance.

I duck behind a cluster of wet bushes in front of a vacant house to pull on my jeans, T-shirt, and hoodie. My socks, which I've had on the whole time, are soaked from the grass, so I peel them off and hang them on a thorny branch before slipping into my Chuck's.

There aren't many cars on the road, but the headlights of the few that pass cast strange shapes on the twisted trees and gutted buildings. Bass thumps from the occasional trunk, and the deep vibrations linger in the ground beneath my feet.

The neighborhood I live in is rundown as hell, but this side of town makes mine look like something to strive toward. Houses torched or boarded up in every direction. The charred remains of a burned-out Ford station wagon sits at the curb like some long dead, prehistoric turtle. Street signs lean, tagged with gang graffiti and pocked with bullet holes. Shattered glass twinkles like tiny constellations on the pavement. Entire streets are losing their fight against nature as grass and scrub and noxious growth all creep back in to reclaim the fringes, where the boundary between city and country has been virtually erased. Every now and then, I see a figure or two on a front porch, visible only by their outlines and the glowing cherries of their cigarettes.

About a block from the drive-thru where Dwight dropped me off earlier, I come upon a woman dressed in dirty sweatpants and a flannel shirt squatting next to a dumpster. She clutches a skinny glass pipe in her hands. Her fingertips are ragged.

"I'll make you cum," she says through blistered lips. Her voice is hoarse, desperate, and she seems to peer right through me, eyes blazing. "Help me out, baby, I'll get you off good. Just gotta get right . . ."

I feel a knot in my chest as I walk on, only once glancing back as she continues to solicit herself.

Shots pop off a couple streets away, followed by the squealing of tires, so I quicken my pace.

When I get to the drive-thru, there are no cars at the window, so I resign myself to going in, hoping for someone to give me a lift.

Inside, a Middle-Eastern man stands behind the counter reading a newspaper and listening to some high-pitched, fluty-sounding music on a small, battery-powered radio that sits on the counter. He looks up when I enter.

My hope that there would be at least one customer in the store fizzles out; apart from me and the proprietor, the place is deserted. He continues staring as I approach the magazine rack and mindlessly flip through an issue of *High Times* and wait for someone to come in.

"Help you, sir?" he asks, placing his palms on the counter and leaning forward to get a better look at me.

"Just looking, thanks."

I place the magazine back on the rack, and as I'm scanning some of the others, there's a sound like static, which I soon identify as the buzzing of flies around a batch of fried chicken in the heated food case beside me.

"This is not library," the man says. "You must buy something or go."

It occurs to me that I'd be better off waiting for someone to roll up to the drive-thru window outside, so I walk toward the door.

"Where you going?" he shouts after me.

As I step back into the damp night, the clerk begins yelling something in what I assume is his native tongue. Around the corner, out of his line of vision, I wait.

After what seems like a long time, I start to get frustrated. But just as I'm about to start walking again, a souped-up Cutlass with an iridescent paint job and obnoxious rear spoiler pulls in. A young Latino guy is driving, and a beautiful girl with braided hair and big gold-hoop earrings, who reminds me a little of Isabelle, sits in the passenger seat puffing on a plastic-tipped cigar.

The car's rimmed wheels roll over the little black cord in the drive-thru and a bell rings inside the store. I walk to the edge of the lot and wait for them to pull away from the window, and just before they turn onto the street, I walk up on the driver's side.

But I realize the error in not announcing myself from farther back, because as soon as I'm up on the car there's a .357 snub-nose inches from my face. I recognize the make of the piece because Mom used to have one just like it before downgrading to a .25 auto—something a little more purse-friendly.

"The fuck you doin', white boy?" the driver says. "You tryin' to get lit the fuck up?"

I back away a few steps, holding my hands up, palms facing him. "Whoa, it's cool, it's cool. I'm just looking for a ride back up the hill, man."

As he assesses me, I get a closer look at him: lines shaved in his eyebrows and a pair of praying hands tattooed on the side of his neck.

"You can't walk up on motherfuckers like that," he says. Then he motions with his gun. "What you got in your pocket."

I look down at the bulge in my hoodie and realize I'm still carrying the apple I grabbed from the fruit bowl this morning. I reach into my pocket slowly and remove it.

"Just an apple," I say, holding it up for him to see. "Like I said, I'm just looking for a ride."

"I don't know," he says, sucking his teeth and putting on an exaggerated display of mulling it over. "Up the hill's a long way, and gas is expensive."

I consider offering to pay him, but then I think about how I got taxed almost thirty dollars at the liquor store when I cashed my check, so I stay quiet.

"What you think, Maria?" he asks his girl. He keeps his eyes and the .357 pointed at me. "Should we give him a ride?"

"I don't know, Hector," she says, flicking the ash of her cigar into the parking lot with one of her long press-on nails, "he looks kinda dangerous to me."

Hector shrugs, his expression telling me his hands are tied. "You heard her," he says. "She thinks you're dangerous."

I'm fed up and don't even bother asking again. Instead, I stuff the apple back in my pocket, and say, "Thanks, anyway."

As I walk away, I can hear them snickering.

Crossing the street I kick a beer bottle that lay in the gutter. It skitters across the asphalt and rolls into a sewer drain.

I'm about a block away when a car approaches me from behind.

"Hey," Hector says, his Cutlass idling at a slow crawl beside me. I don't answer him. "Hey," he says again. When

I finally stop, he stops, and when I looked at him, leaned back in his seat with his hand propped up on the steering wheel, he says, "Damn, we was just fuckin' with you, white boy. Shit, you take a motherfucker too seriously. Jump in."

The inside of the car smells like Maria's Black & Mild, weed, and vanilla. There's a yellow pine tree-shaped air freshener dangling from the rearview mirror along with a plastic rosary, and some sort of Spanish hip-hop coming through the rear speakers.

Maria lights a blunt and passes it to me. I take a hit, fill my lungs, and hold my breath as we cruise over the bridge and across the river. I'm still holding it as we climb our way out of the valley on the other side.

#

Standing beside the house, I can hear them inside arguing, muffled voices getting louder and louder with each exchange. The duffel bag is at my feet. As I listen, a glass shatters against a wall.

A sudden sense of indecision has me feeling as though I'm standing knee-deep in wet cement or the sands of some sea-choked shoreline. My body and mind are at odds. Nearly all my instincts are tangled and tugging in opposite directions. I turn my head toward the rush of the highway running just out of sight, beyond a steep slope across the road. I ask myself if this is it, and if so, why can't I just go already.

"Just go," I say to myself, not much above a whisper.

The shouting rises, growing clearer as Frank and Mom move their fight into the front room, and I watch as their silhouettes act out their endless drama on the dirty curtains.

It occurs to me that the reason I haven't left yet is that maybe I'm looking for a reason to stay. And I'm not sure why that would be other than maybe I'm afraid.

I had told myself that if Isabelle begged me not to go—as unlikely as that would be—I would go anyway. But that's as big of a lie as I've ever told. All afternoon I was wishing that she'd tell me to stay, thinking perhaps it would be a sign that what we had really was something more than we said it was. But in the end, it was just a kiss, a casual invitation to hit her up if I decide to stick around, and what? A necklace.

I took off the Saint Christopher medallion after leaving her house and put it in my pocket because, at the time, instead of thinking the gesture was endearing, I just thought it was silly, a token of her faith in fairytales. But thinking now, maybe it was also a gesture of her faith in me. Maybe she believed I was making the right decision, even if I wasn't sure myself.

I take the necklace out and run my thumb over the medal's raised impression as the cheap, tarnished chain lay draped over my knuckles.

The shouting inside the house has died down now, and my legs no longer feel so heavy, so I creep over the porch rail and peer in through the split in the curtains.

What I see is something I'll never claim to comprehend: They sit embracing on the sofa, Mom's head nestled in the groove of Frank's collarbone, his hand stroking her hair. They look like the world's happiest couple.

I tell myself it's only half-time.

You can't change the wind, my grandfather says, and a moment of clarity comes over me. Taking it as my cue, I climb off the porch, sling the duffel over my shoulder, and loop Saint Christopher, patron saint of weary travelers, over my head. Maybe it's silly, maybe it isn't. Either way, it never hurts to have someone watching your back.

When I approach the end of the street, the murmurs and clacks of people talking and shooting pool inside the Hilltop Tavern drift out into the night air. Some old country singer, mourning lost love, croons from the juke, and I'm momentarily struck by the way the neon Pabst sign sheds its gaseous glow across the sidewalk, how it makes the weeds poking through the cracks of the buckled pavement look like fire.

My stomach gurgles, and for the first time today I'm hungry. I remove the apple from my pocket, breathe on it, and rub it on my shirt, because that's what people do sometimes. I take a bite. A drop of juice runs down my chin and I wipe it away with my sleeve, savoring the sweet taste. Without looking back, I adjust my sails, and after a moment the wind picks up, moving me toward the on-ramp, toward the surging sound of passing cars.

Talking and Standing Still

Our washer at home still worked, but the dryer was busted, so once a week my wife and me loaded the back of our Chevette with baskets of soggy laundry and headed down the street to Dirty Dungarees to have a couple beers. Some bright mind had years ago got the notion to open a Laundromat with a full-service bar inside. I'd had a similar idea once, only mine involved combining a video store with a pizza parlor. Order a pie, look for a movie while you wait was my thinking. They've got a whole chain of those now, and I had nothing to do with it. Million-dollar idea and all I did was talk, talk, talk.

I'd had lots of ideas. For instance, the mini-van with the sliding doors on both sides? Came up with that gem back in the 80s, damn near twenty years before they started making them. Mayonnaise in the squeeze bottle? Yep, that was me too.

Anyway, my wife and me—Sharon was her name—we were sitting in a booth in the bar with a half empty pitcher of beer between us on the sticky tabletop. There was a glass partition separating the bar room and the Laundromat, so we could see our clothes tumbling behind the dryers' circular windows. When they stopped for the second time, I acted as if to go check them. They'd been dry the first time, of course, but I kept sticking more quarters in, just the same. We weren't finished drinking yet. My suspicion was it was the only thing that allowed Sharon to tolerate my presence by that point in the marriage.

So I went and plunked in about another half hour's worth of silver. And wouldn't you know it, when I returned to the booth, some knucklehead was in my seat slurring about *I want to write you a poem* to Sharon while she egged him on with a coy smile and a series of *Oh, you* hand gestures.

Now, I'm not much for conflict, and I wasn't all that threatened, so I sat at the end of the bar and listened while the idiot fawned all over her.

After a bit, though, Sharon turned in her seat and said, "Damn it, Marty, how come you never write me poems? This nice fella wants to write me a poem. What do you think about that?"

I said, "What's to think?"

"All that talkin' you do, I imagine it wouldn't kill you to write me a poem once in a while is all I'm sayin'."

Looking back on it, if I was any kind of a man at all, I'd have gotten up and put that drunk bastard on his ass, or at least said something in my own defense. But instead I ordered a bottle of Bud, just sat there picking at the edges of the label, not saying a thing to either of them.

There'd always been men offering her the moon. Sharon was a fine-looking woman, and I suppose she deserved to be flattered now and then. How she'd ended up with me, she often reflected, was some kind of freak accident, had to be, one she was resigned to but still trying to figure out. And maybe that's precisely why we were still together: neither of us was much good at anything besides talking.

There hadn't even been any real flirtations between us that first night in the gloom of Miller's Tap. Just a few passing glances and a run-in at the jukebox. "Play something slow," she'd said. "Something to drown my heart."

So I punched in Willie's "Blue Eyes Crying in the Rain" and watched her dance with herself in the dim light.

Even then I just stood still, watching as life went by.

Anyhow, by now the poet had moved from my seat in the booth and was now sitting at the bar scribbling his ode on a cocktail napkin. He appeared hard at work, almost desperate about it, like it was something his life depended on, and the fact that I couldn't think of a single time when I'd ever put that much effort into anything, well, it hollowed me out a little.

Sharon was still turned sideways in her seat, tapping her lacquered nails on the table and looking at me like someone might observe a curious insect pinned on a wall. Her eyes followed me as I reclaimed my seat across from her. She smiled, a half grin that stated the truth of things before she even opened her mouth.

"You oughta start appreciating me more," she said. "Because someday the right wind is gonna blow through, and I'll be gone."

Now, could be that I was stubborn, or maybe just a fool—hell, could be that I still am—but I didn't know what I needed to do just then. Specifics, I mean. I've never been real good at reading between the lines. Yeah, the obvious thing would be to come right out and ask. But, well, that's the thing about words—sometimes when you need them the most they just don't come. Even when they're clear and articulate in your mind, it's like they get lost on the way to your lips.

After several minutes of me avoiding her eyes for fear that the remaining threads of what we had holding us together would snap, she got up and grabbed her purse. "And that's exactly what I'm getting at," she said. "Nothing to say for yourself." Then she stormed off toward the ladies' room.

So there I was, alone in the booth. The poet had passed out on the bar rail. I went over and stood beside him, and when I looked over, I saw the napkin he'd been toiling over. A mess of illegible scrawls that bled away into nothing where they met the side of his sweaty glass.

I ordered another beer, and for a moment I felt a sense of triumph, witnessing how he'd failed. But even then, I think I knew on some level that his failure was also mine. And like his words, I'd soon bleed away into nothing too.

The Bad Ones

It was the second week of June, and the sun hung blazing in the clear blue sky. School had just let out for the summer, and as the four boys walked along the top of the ridge, David Wallace could already tell it was going to be a long couple of months. With him were Nate Griggs, his weirdo younger brother, Rodney, and a husky kid named Lucas Hoffstetter who all the kids called Chubs. Nate, a lanky boy with big gums and stiff spiky hair like the bristles on a hog, was fourteen, older than the others by two years, which he believed put him in charge. And although David received his share of Nate's bullying, it was Chubs who bore the brunt of everything Nate dished out. One of Nate's favorite things to do was spit onto his fingertips and fling it at people. He'd call, "Hey, Chubs, come check it out," and when the younger boy came running, Nate would spin around and let him have it. His aim was good, too. One time he'd gotten him right in the eye while Chubs was on his bike. The poor kid wrecked into a fencepost before hitting the asphalt and skinning up his knees and elbows. Nate just laughed and said, "Ride much?" then wandered off with Rodney following at his heels like a dumb, faithful mutt.

Chubs was about the closest thing David had to a real friend, and it bugged him the way the older boy always picked on him. He asked Chubs all the time when he was going to stop falling for the same stupid trick, but Chubs always just shrugged and looked at his feet.

When they came to the narrow path on the far side of the blighted field atop the ridge, they followed it single-file through a mess of brambles and into a stand of tall oaks toward their camp, which sat in a small clearing of packed earth just above the bend in Trapper's Creek. Just off to one side of it was the tepee they had constructed the day before with some thick, fallen tree branches and a tattered tarp pulled from the trash pile in the woods down behind old man Pruitt's place. The site overlooked the town but was well hidden among the thick summer foliage. When they had first found the place in early spring, before the leaves all came in, it had been a lot more exposed. Now it felt like they could see the world, even though the world couldn't see them, which must be sort of what God feels like, David thought.

"We need a fire," Nate said. He pointed at David. "You and Chubs go find us some wood. We'll finish gettin' things set up here."

Rather than question Nate's commands, David knew it was better to just agree, so he and Chubs wandered off into the woods to gather things to burn. When they came back about ten minutes later with armloads of sticks and small dead logs, Nate was just finishing up stacking rocks and pieces of broken cinderblock, forming a jagged ring in the dirt. Rodney sat off to the side hacking at an old spray-paint can with a dull hatchet head. He grunted with each downward motion, drooling down the front of his shirt. The boy went to school with the rest of them, but he was in the special class. He and a handful of other boys and girls spent their days in a battered old trailer out behind the school.

David always wondered, when he'd look out his classroom window and see the kids being led from the cafeteria back to the trailer, what they could be teaching them in there, because if Rodney was any example, David figured it sure couldn't be much.

Rodney had hardly talked since a few summers ago, when Nate had convinced him to hold a lit M-80 between his teeth on the fourth of July. When it exploded, it had taken Rodney's bottom lip clean off, along with half of the top one, and cracked his bottom front teeth just above the gum-line. He tried to hide the fact, but David found the kid hard to look at most of the time, especially on the occasions that he did try to talk. Any words that required the letters p, b, v, m, w, or a "th" sound came out unintelligible and were always followed by a bubbly strand of spit that oozed over the broken stumps in his lower jaw.

Although Rodney had always been a little loose in the head, the firecracker incident seemed to make what screws he had left come unthreaded, and now the boy just wasn't right—that much was certain.

"Give me them matches you got," Nate said.

David pulled out a book of matches he'd swiped from his mom's work earlier that day when her back was turned. He wasn't sure why he took them, just that he probably wasn't supposed to, which always made him want to do things even more for some reason.

His mom tended bar at Miller's Tap during the day and worked the nightshift cooking at a place called The

Cloverleaf over by the turnpike. "I know I ain't around as much as I oughta be," she often said as she was heading out the door, "but it's the only way to keep up on bills and put a little aside so we can get out of this godforsaken town someday." His good-for-nothing father had run off when David was still in diapers, and for as long as he could remember, his mom had worked two, sometimes three jobs, which left him to fend for himself most nights. So whenever she let him come to the Tap when she was working, he jumped at the chance. Sometimes he'd spend her whole shift shooting pool and drinking Cokes and playing songs on the jukebox.

But during the summer, his mom encouraged him to enjoy being outside. "I don't want you hangin' around in here with these old drunks," she had told him just this morning when he stopped in to ask her if he could have a pop and shoot a game. She poured him a Coke and said, "You finish that up and go on out and play. Enjoy being young, 'cause it'll be over before you know it. Ain't that right, Sam?"

One of the old men at the end of the bar downed the last of his draft. "I know that's right," he said, taking a long drag from his cigarette and staring into his empty mug, as if maybe his lost youth was somewhere at the bottom.

"Come back before my shift ends," his mom said, "and I'll fix you something to eat."

He finished his Coke, and as he crossed the parking lot on his bike, heading back toward home, David ran into Nate and Rodney in the alley behind Mort's Little Shopper and decided to pedal over to see what they were up to. Nate was sucking on a Blow-Pop, his entire mouth shiny and red, while Rodney poked at the bloated carcass of a dead cat with a bent coat hanger. The cat was covered in tiny red ants, thousands of them, and looked like it had been there about a week, maybe more. David figured it must have gotten run over. He liked cats. They were mysterious and didn't slobber all over your face like dogs. He wondered if it had belonged to anyone, and as he stared at the moving red mass swarming all over the cat's face and body, David also found himself wondering if the poor thing had died fast or slow.

#

After getting some twigs going with a couple fistfuls of wadded-up newspaper from the trash pile, Nate ordered Chubs to add some of the bigger pieces of wood. He complied, but snuffed out the flames as he tried to stack the logs.

"Dammit, Chubs, you fucked it up," Nate said, walking around him and kicking him in the back with one of his ratty off-brand sneakers. Chubs fell forward into the pit with a thud and a grunt, burning the palm of his right hand in the smoldering ashes.

"What the hell, Nate," David said, "What'd you have to do that for?"

David stood up and went over to Chubs, who was sitting in the dirt on the edge of the site, crying and holding his burned hand to his chest.

"Fat ass can't do nothin' right," Nate said.

"I think you hurt him real bad this time."

Nate shot a stream of spit through the gap in his crooked front teeth into the fire pit. It hissed like a snake. "He's just being a pussy," he said.

"You all right, Chubs?" David knelt down beside him.

Chubs nodded, sniffling. "Yeah, I think so."

"He'd be fine if you'd quit kissin' his ass all the time," Nate said. He picked up a stone and threw it, as if skipping it across water, directly above their heads. It bounced off several trees and made a series of hollow cracking sounds as it disappeared down the hill. David ducked after the rock had already whizzed by them and swung around to look at Nate.

"What?" Nate said, chuckling. "You gonna do somethin'?"

David sat down in the dirt next to Chubs without saying anything. He went back and forth inside his head, wishing that Nate would just go away and scolding himself for continuing to hang around the kid in the first place. He glanced over at his friend. He had stopped crying, but his scrunched-up face made it look like he might start again. Chubs needed him, David thought then. That's why he still hung around. David was no match for Nate—the kid outweighed him by nearly twenty pounds and was a few inches taller—but he at least spoke up when Nate got too rough. And when he was around, Nate usually let up on

Chubs after a while. There's no telling what he'd put the kid through if David wasn't there.

"This sucks," Nate said. "We ain't got no more paper."

Just then there was a sound like air being let out of a bike tire as Rodney punctured the spray-can with the hatchet. Everyone looked over at him. His scarred face was colored by a blue mist of paint. He got excited and used the hatchet to pry the can open, pulling the marble out and staring at it like it was some sort of priceless jewel.

"C'mon, Rodney," Nate said. "Let's get out of here. I'm hungry anyways." Rodney jumped up and shoved the marble into his pocket, and as the brothers headed toward the path, Nate shouted back, "See you fags later!" Then he laughed and trotted off through the woods with Rodney close behind him.

David and Chubs sat there in silence for a few minutes. There were still several hours of daylight left, but some dark clouds had moved in from the north. Chubs said, "He didn't mean nothing by it. He was just playin' around."

David looked through the trees, out past the old abandoned high school sitting like an ancient ruin in a sea of weeds and cracked asphalt, to where a plume of black smoke rose up from somewhere across town. It was probably someone burning tires or trash. He wanted to tell Chubs he was as stupid as Rodney if he actually believed Nate was just kidding around. Instead, he nudged him in the arm and pointed toward the smoke in the distance. "Looks like someone got their fire goin'," he said, and they both laughed.

235

#

Although he had put up with Nate's meanness in varying degrees since the first grade, it never failed to surprise David just how rotten he could be. As if spitting on Chubs, beating up on him, and calling him names wasn't enough, Nate always came up with new ways to torture the boy. David suffered small in comparison. He had a thicker skin than Chubs, could shrug it off when the older boy punched him or flicked him in the nuts or made filthy remarks about his mom. But Chubs was the perfect victim because he took the abuse and kept coming back. It reminded David of some of the guys his mom ran around with over the years, guys who would get drunk and treat her like garbage, but for some strange reason she'd stay with them like they were something worth holding on to. Once, she had woken up to find the guy long gone and the jar where she kept their escape fund, in the cupboard above the refrigerator, empty of all but a few sticky nickels crusted to the bottom. But without fail some new bozo always came into the picture to replace the old one. Some days, David resented his mother for allowing herself to be treated like that, but others he just felt bad that no one ever loved her back the way she loved them.

Now it seemed he felt the same way about his friend. Chubs was a nice kid. Never hurt or spoke ill of anyone. He'd give you his last dollar if you needed it, probably the shoes off his feet. But people like Nate Griggs seemed to regard those with kind natures as weak and were inclined to exploit their weakness at every turn. David thought this might very well be the reason behind there being so many awful people in the world: because the good ones are too good to withstand the bad ones. It was like some sort of terrible natural order that, no matter how hard he tried, he just couldn't understand. What David did understand was that Nate knew Chubs would never fight back, which made him easy prey. More than once, David actually caught himself being angry with Chubs for being such a coward. But he knew it was wrong to be mad at Chubs, and such thoughts eventually made David wonder if maybe he was one of the bad ones, too, just for thinking them.

#

It was the end of June when Nate decided that they were a lost tribe. He had come up with the idea one morning when he and Rodney found a sparrow with a broken wing on the side of the road. David and Chubs were already at the site when the two arrived. Rodney had the twitching bird cupped in his grimy hands. "From now on, we're Indians," Nate said. "We'll earn feathers for different things, like gettin' firewood and standin' guard and stuff." Rodney put the bird down on a piece of the cinderblock around the fire pit, its feet kicking. He pulled the hatchet head from his back pocket and, using the blunt side, hammered the bird's tiny skull until it was nothing but a little glob of jelly with a beak sticking out.

Nate took the bird from his little brother and started pulling out its brown and white feathers, shoving them in the pocket of his cut-offs. "I'll assign jobs," he said. "David, you go to the trash pile, get some extra paper for burnin' and find us something to use for headbands to put the feathers in. Rodney, you go with him, see if there's anything else we can use. Me and Chubs'll get wood and start the fire with the little bit of paper we still got. After, we'll all get our first feather. Now get goin'."

At first, as he and Rodney moved down the hill through the woods, David thought playing Indians was sort of dumb. Kids' stuff. But he was more curious as to why Nate would have Chubs stay behind to help with the fire. Ever since the day he kicked him into the pit, he hadn't put Chubs on fire duty once. Usually Rodney stayed with Nate, and the change in routine worried David a little.

As Rodney scurried ahead of him, David tried to convince himself that Nate hadn't actually been too bad today, other than a few insults, which David was so used to by now that he hardly even noticed anymore. Besides, he supposed that pretending to be Indians might end up being kind of fun, after all.

#

With the zoning being fairly lax this far from the city, a lot of people lived off of the main route of the garbage pick-up. So rather than having to constantly haul it to the dump just outside of town themselves, some folks just let the trash pile up out back. Once in a while, when it got to falling over or stinking too bad, they would set it ablaze and start a new pile in the old one's ashes. The pile in the woods out behind old man Pruitt's little shack was enormous— probably fifty feet around at the bottom and at least ten feet high, David guessed. There wasn't much food waste, however, just some crusty soup cans and a whole bunch of small animal bones. Most of the pile consisted of stuff that David was pretty sure could be junked for money if you were willing to load it up and cart it over to the scrap yard— things like radiators and water heaters, bent screen-doors with the screens busted out, old grills and bed frames. There were dozens of rusted tire rims, sheets of tin, machine parts, an old dented ice chest with a family of possums living inside. David would sometimes see guys driving around town, stopping at the curbs in front of houses and rooting through dumpsters, loading up the backs of their trucks with stuff like that, trucks he'd later see parked in the gravel lot of Miller's Tap, the backs empty of all but some discarded jugs of antifreeze or motor oil, the occasional spare tire.

David used to see Mr. Pruitt in town about once a week, coming out of Mort's with a sack of potatoes, or going into Kurtzal's Hardware, but he had seen less and less of the old man over the last couple of years, heard his wife had died and his only son had gone crazy or something. Now he was supposedly all alone out here in these woods.

Rooting around, David found a pair of yellowed curtains that he figured they could tear into strips for headbands and some more newspaper for the fire. Rodney had grabbed up a soggy spool of twine, a few bungee cords, and some long strands of rusty barbed wire that were coiled around the legs of an old wringer washing machine. He held them up for David to see, and a shiny string of drool hung from his mouth as he tried to twist his damaged face into something like a smile.

When they got back to the top of the hill, there was no fire, just some twigs in the pit and a few fungus-covered logs lying off to the side. David looked around for Nate and Chubs and was just about to holler for them when they came out of the tepee, ducking under the naked corpse of the little bird, which Nate had hung by a string from the door. The older boy was scratching his crotch and David noticed that Chubs's eyes were red and puffy. When he asked him what was wrong, Chubs told him it was just his allergies acting up, but David knew he'd been crying again because of something Nate had done. He just wasn't sure what it was.

"Took you queers long enough," Nate said. "What'd you get?"

David and Rodney dropped the supplies on the ground, and as Nate walked over to examine the haul, David said, "I thought you were gonna build a fire." He glanced over at Chubs, who was chewing on a hangnail and staring at his shoes like he always did when he was nervous or avoiding something.

"Wasn't enough paper, after all," Nate replied. "Had to wait for you to get back with some more. Chubs decided we should go in and make sure the tepee was secure. Didn't you, Chubs?"

Chubs didn't say a word, just nodded without looking up and busied himself picking up more twigs.

#

It was mid-July when Nate first tied Chubs to the tree. He said being a tribe of Indians wasn't much fun without enemies, so he made Chubs his personal captive. By then Nate had plucked the sparrow bare and gathered some crow feathers he'd found throughout the woods, fashioned himself a headdress, and he demanded that everyone call him Chief.

At first he just left Chubs there, tied up at the bottom of the hill for a couple hours at a time. "He'll be a warning to others who might try to attack," Nate said, getting a bit too into the game as far David was concerned. Chubs actually seemed to enjoy his new role, however, even giggling from time to time, and since it wasn't hurting him any, David decided to play along. That first time, as evening came on, Nate got bored and told David, "Go untie the prisoner." By the time they returned to camp, Chubs looked exhausted and was no longer giggling, and Nate and Rodney had already gone home. Even though David felt they had left him down there far too long, Chubs insisted he didn't mind.

"That was fun," he said, sounding weary and staggering a little as they walked back along the path together.

David looked west just as the sun dropped out of sight. "If you say so," he said. "Don't seem like much fun to me."

"How come you keep playin' then?" Chubs asked.

It was the same question David had been asking himself all summer. But rather than tell Chubs the real reason—that he needed to protect him from Nate—he just said, "I don't know. I guess I just ain't got nothin' better to do."

"Well, I'm glad you keep playin' still." Chubs said.

David again wondered how far Nate would go if he wasn't around to speak up for Chubs. Then he thought he was giving himself more credit than he deserved. "Yeah, I suppose it ain't so bad," he said. He tried to believe the lie, assured himself that today could have been worse. After all, at least no one got hurt.

It was sometime around midsummer that David began lying awake in bed at night, trying to talk to God. He and his mom never went to church because she believed most of the so-called Christians that filed into St. John's or the Providence Presbyterian across town on Sundays were nothing but a bunch of no-good hypocrites. She had told him this one afternoon while they were on their way to the More for Less Market in Middleton to do some grocery shopping. He'd asked her, "How come we don't ever go to church or nothin'?"

As they passed the church, she pointed to a group of men standing out front. They all had greased-back hair and dress shirts tucked into their dungarees, some smoking cigarettes, others chewing tobacco and spitting in the grass. "You see those men there?" she said. David nodded. "They call themselves Christians, but they're just a bunch of drunks who like to beat on their wives." She paused for a moment, then said, "They ain't no Christians."

David looked confused. "But they're at church."

His mom looked at him and patted his knee. "Oh, sweetheart, that don't mean nothin'. You just treat people good, and try to help those who can't help themselves. In the end, that's really all God wants us to do." Then she lit one of her long menthol cigarettes, exhaled a trail of thick blue smoke from the corner of her mouth, and didn't say another word on the subject.

David didn't give it much thought after that. Every now and then, he'd say a feeble prayer when he heard his mom and whatever joker she was with at the time fighting. But to David, it seemed that God never really answered, anyway. Must be too busy, he told himself. The world's a big place.

But one night, in the dark of his bedroom, he just started talking, hoping someone was listening. He thought about what his mom had said about being a good person and helping people. He stared at the ceiling and prayed. He asked God if that was really all he had to do.

David waited for an answer to his question. But night after night, as he lay there listening to the soft ebb and flow of his own breath, the only reply he got was from an occasional car backfiring somewhere in the surrounding countryside as he drifted off to sleep.

The days grew hotter and hotter, and on the first Saturday of August, David's mom took him over to the Village Outlet thrift store in Youngstown, which was about a thirty-minute drive from Miles Junction each way. She wanted him to pick out some clothes for the upcoming school year. Afterward, she took him to an all-you-can-eat buffet, where he ate so many mashed potatoes and dishes of soft-serve ice cream that he was groaning in the car and took a nap on the couch when they got back home.

When he woke up two hours later it was nearly 8:00, and his mom had already left for her shift at the Cloverleaf. The air inside their dilapidated ranch-style was thick and stale. His shirt was damp with sweat and clung to him like flypaper. He had told Chubs that he would sleep over at his house tonight, so he rubbed his eyes and picked up the phone.

The boy's senile grandmother, who Chubs had lived with ever since his folks died in a car wreck when he was still in kindergarten, told David he wasn't home. "I s'pect he's out playin' somewhere with that nice boy," she told him, "one with the funny lookin' brother."

David thanked her and hung up the receiver, then walked out on the stoop. The air here wasn't much better. The sky was hazy, and everything seemed wilted. He wasn't used to napping in the middle of the day and was groggy as he crossed the road, jumping the shallow ditch and making his way through the field toward the ridge.

When he got to the site, the fire pit was smoking but no one was around. The woods were silent except for a few twittering birds and some mosquitoes. The patch of sky visible through the trees had grown darker, and a faint thunder rumbled inside an approaching clot of dense storm clouds. He checked the tepee. The decaying sparrow still hung in the entrance, crawling with squirming white things that, for a moment, reminded David of the Rice Crispies he'd had for breakfast that morning.

When he stepped back outside, a sharp whistling sound, followed closely by a loud crack, like a gunshot, echoed up from the bottom of the hill, and David jumped. He staggered, colliding with the dead bird. He cringed and moved away from it. After about a minute, again: *whistle— crack!* But this time, as the echo subsided, Nate's vicious laugh rose up through the woods. David feared the worst, and without thinking descended the hill as fast as he could, losing his traction and sliding on his backside in the dirt and shale.

They came into view before he reached the bottom. A few yards from the water, Chubs sat on the ground, bound to the tree with twine and bungee cords, one leg bent under him, the other one kicked out to the side. He had been stripped down to his underwear, which were dingy and soaked.

"Please, Nate, this ain't fun no more," Chubs begged, tears cutting clean tracks down his cheeks. The older boy was shirtless and wearing his crude headdress of sparrow and crow feathers. He'd streaked his own face with mud and soot to look like war paint. He paced in front of Chubs, cackling and whipping the crying boy across his pudgy belly with a long switch. Thin red welts hash-marked his doughy skin. Between every few lashes, Nate lit one of the bottle rockets he had saved from the holiday. He'd arranged them in a semi-circle, sticking out of the dirt and pointed toward Chubs.

They were positioned in such a way as to just miss his face, but several of them had hit him straight on—a few in the chest and shoulder, one in the side of the neck—leaving black powder burns. Rodney hid behind the muddy clump of an uprooted tree that had fallen across the creek, covering his ears, and cowering lower to the ground each time one of the firecrackers exploded.

By the time David got there, Chubs was a blubbering mess, unable to even beg anymore. Nate was too preoccupied to interpret Rodney's lipless babbles of warning and didn't hear David running up behind him until it was too late. When his ears finally seemed to register the sound of dry branches snapping under David's feet, David was already on top of him, knocking Nate face-first into the dirt, the headdress flying from his head.

"You sonofabitch!" David screamed.

They grappled on the ground. Nate was stunned, but only for a few moments. Within seconds, he'd gained control and resumed his mad laughter. Nate straddled him, pinning David's shoulders with his knees. He shoved a fistful of dirt and leaves into David's mouth. "Big mistake, faggot," Nate said, slapping David across the face. "Never interfere with the interrogation of a captive."

David spat, trying not to choke. His heart slammed against the inside of his chest. "You're a crazy fucker," he gasped, struggling to breathe beneath Nate's weight.

Rodney kept peeking over the fallen log and ducking back down, expecting another explosion.

"The only mother I fucked was yours." Nate grinned down at David with his crooked teeth. Beads of greasy sweat broke and ran down from his ash-smeared forehead, dripping onto David's face.

David continued to struggle as Nate reached for the filthy headdress that had been knocked off. He turned it in his hands, as if to make sure it hadn't been damaged, then placed it back on his head.

David prayed. He couldn't think of much besides *Please God Please God*, but he figured God would have to understand.

Unfortunately, it seemed that the Almighty was once again too busy.

David gathered enough air in his lungs to force the words, "This ain't—how you play a game—Nate."

Nate leaned in close and exhaled a sour breath. He lit the mini-Bic lighter he'd been using and held the flame about an inch from David's left eye and said, "It's *Chief* to you, boy."

Suddenly the sky lit up, and there was another crack from far above the trees, much louder than the others and without the preceding whistle.

Nate jumped to his feet and drove a fist into David's stomach, a blow that spread through his body and caused him to curl into a ball. As David lay there, clutching himself, Nate went over and whispered something in Chubs's ear. Then he hopped onto the fallen tree and crossed the creek where Rodney was still huddled like a scared puppy. The brothers disappeared through the brush. Chubs sat strapped to the tree, his head slumped to one side, his chest heaving. As David crawled toward him, there was another flash of light and a clap of thunder. Seconds later, the clouds split open.

#

On the way back from the creek, Chubs asked him in a weak voice if he'd still spend the night. David just wanted to go home, so he asked if Chubs wanted to stay at his place instead. Chubs said sure. "Can we just stop at my house for some dry clothes and to see if Grandma's okay?" he asked. He worried about her sometimes, what with her being so old and all.

David nodded. "Yeah, we can do that."

A little while later, after making some TV dinners and playing the Nintendo Chubs had brought from his house until just past midnight, David offered him the lumpy bed. But the boy said he liked the floor, so he laid out some old quilts and a couple throw pillows from the couch. They were silent for a while. Finally, David said, "Nate whispered something to you. What'd he say?" When Chubs didn't respond, he looked down at him; he was already asleep, squeezing one of the pillows to his chest like a shield.

David lay there listening to the rain and watching shadows dance across the walls. He couldn't get it out of his mind: the image of Chubs bound to that tree, terrified and begging for his life. And Nate's beady eyes. The way he

248

laughed like it was the most fun he'd ever had. How he leaned in close with the cigarette lighter. *It's Chief to you, boy.*

He didn't bother praying anymore. It didn't work, he told himself, not even when it really mattered. Instead he rolled over on his side and watched rain overflow from the clogged gutters outside his window.

Around three in the morning, he woke up when he heard his mom come in. She wasn't alone. There were hushing sounds as she and the man she was with crept past his door toward her room. Soon, the bed began squeaking, then the moaning and heavy breathing. He put his head under his pillow like he always did and tried not to think about how it would turn out, though he knew: In the morning, the guy would act all buddy-buddy with him while his mom made them all breakfast, something fancy like French toast or eggs Benedict. He would maybe ask David if he'd like to go fishing sometime or help him fix-up an old car or go see the new Schwarzenegger flick. Maybe the guy would stick around for a week or two. But probably not.

The rain continued to tap its fingers on the sheet-metal roof. David let the sound lull him back to sleep. He pictured Nate with those grimy feathers sticking up around his head. He pictured the murderous look in his eyes. Soon, darkness stole the image, and his last conscious thought was that the fucker had to pay.

#

Chubs slept over at David's for several days. They spent hours playing video games and watching movies on the little television in the living room while David's mom was at work. She'd come home before her night shift and fix them some macaroni & cheese or frozen pizza for supper. Chubs didn't talk about the day by the creek. In fact, he didn't talk about much at all other that not wanting to go back to school in two weeks. "Sometimes I wish I could just never go to school again," he said one afternoon. But David was lost in thought, trying to figure out how he could pay Nate back for what he had done.

A few minutes later, he asked Chubs again what he'd tried to ask him before: "What did Nate whisper to you that day?"

Chubs started biting his fingernails, avoiding the question. His eyes became wet, and he looked like he was trying not to blink so he wouldn't cry.

"Come on, tell me," David said.

After another minute of hesitation, Chubs started to cry, but his face was flat, expressionless. He spoke in a low voice, as if to himself. "He said to never tell no one." Chubs paused, looked down and away, then added, "Or next time'll be a lot worse."

#

The rain stayed steady, and when it finally stopped the following Saturday, it was followed by a week-long stretch of oppressive humidity that left people feeling slick and ready for fall. Nate hadn't come around to David's house, and from what Chubs had told him over the phone, he hadn't come by there, either.

So David began watching Nate from a distance, hoping to catch him alone and off-guard somehow.

One morning, as David reached the top of Cherry Street on his bicycle, he looked down into the trailer park, which sat across Route 70 from the overgrown field that ran all the way back to Trapper's Creek, and Nate was standing on the sagging front steps of their dented old single-wide while his pot-bellied old man chewed on a cigar and talked to some serious-looking guy in a suit. Rodney sat in the backseat of a long black car, staring out the window, off into space somewhere. David wondered where that man was taking him as he watched him get into the car and drive away. Rodney turned to look out the back window, looking confused, as if he was wondering the same thing.

David still didn't know what he was going to do, even after thinking on it for quite a while. But when he spotted Nate crossing the field on the ridge that night before suppertime, he decided that whatever it was, the site was where it had to happen.

#

David found Nate chucking rocks through windows out behind the old high school the next afternoon. He was alone, and before he was completely aware of what he was doing, David began walking toward him. "Well, well," Nate said. "Look who it is."

David tried to act as if nothing had ever happened. "What's up, Nate?" Nate ignored him and threw another rock at the school. A window shattered. David said, "I swiped some beers from the fridge at home." It had come out of nowhere; he just blurted it out.

Nate stopped midway through hurling another stone. "Oh, yeah?"

David ran with it. "Yeah, took 'em up to the site. Haven't been up there in a while."

"Thought you and your little girlfriend ran away together" Nate said. He spit at David's feet.

David wanted to jump on him right then, shove one of those rocks down his throat. Instead he said, "Wanna go up?"

Nate considered it for a moment. "What the hell, why not?" He threw the rock he was still holding and looked at David. "But they better be fuckin' cold."

#

When they got there, Nate said, "Well, where they at?"

"In the tepee," David said, his voice quavering slightly.

For a split second, Nate gave him a suspicious look, but then he ducked inside beneath the bird, which still hung by a string but by now was little more than a small cage of hollow bones.

David picked up a triangular piece of cinderblock from the fire ring and approached the doorway of the tepee. His heart beat in his fingers and toes.

"There ain't no fuckin' beers in here," Nate said from inside.

He was afraid he'd lose his nerve, but as Nate ducked under the bird again on his way out of the tepee, David brought the rock down on him where his neck met the base of his skull, and Nate dropped with a thud, his legs still partway inside.

He had hoped to knock him out, but Nate was still moving. Disoriented but moving. So David grabbed a rotten log and hit him again. There was a flurry of bugs as the wood split into pieces. This time, Nate went still.

#

The headdress was hanging from a rusty nail hammered into the side of an oak tree, and David stuffed it in his waistband before getting to work.

Nate was heavy, and it took David several minutes to drag his unconscious but breathing body to the lip of the hill. From there he rolled him down, every now and then having to jostle him around a mess of roots or fallen deadwood.

It took all of his strength to pull Nate across the carpet of matted leaves and mossy stones once they reached the bottom. He got him to the tree, caught his breath, and knuckled sweat from his stinging eyes. He stood over Nate, wondering what to do next.

He stripped Nate's clothing, tossing it aside, leaving him in nothing but his piss-stained briefs. The hardest thing was keeping Nate upright as he sat him at the base of the cottonwood and tied his upper body to its trunk with the scraps of frayed rope and stretched-out bungees that lay scattered on the ground. But he managed to get the job done.

He removed the stinky headdress from his pants and walked over to the edge of the creek. He considered tossing it in, letting the current carry it away, but something told him not to. So he put it on his head and waited.

He saw the first twitch work its way back into Nate's limbs about an hour later. David stood a few feet from him, holding a four-foot switch. He swung it back and forth a few times, listening to it cut through the air. He held an end in each hand, bending it, testing its strength.

Nate groaned. He started to raise his head, his eyes still closed, mouth slack-jawed. David paced before him, dragging the thin branch along the ground beside him. After a moment, Nate's eyes opened. He blinked several times, his brow wrinkled, and finally a look of recognition crept into his face.

David stepped forward, leaned in close, and spoke in a ragged whisper right against his ear: "Hi'ya, Chief." Then he pulled back to see the boy's eyes. He liked it, what he saw there, and smiled as he reached toward him, placing a steady hand on Nate's bare shoulder.

In Just the Right Light

It's about five o'clock when Quentin picks me up, and Julia stands outside the passenger window of his Yukon, her jeans and gloves covered in dirt. She's been working in the garden, raking and pulling weeds. We've been staying with her folks for a while now, and she tries to help out. Her mom's in the house, her old man on the back forty running the brush hog somewhere down by the creek. Quentin's behind the wheel making a big show of it, crossing his heart, raising his right hand as he swears to Julia that everything will be fine. He'll get me home in one piece.

"He's in good hands," he says. "Scouts honor."

She eyes him for a second and turns to me. A look that makes me promise. She's always liked Quentin, or tolerated him because that's the kind of person she is, but I know she worries when we get together, especially now.

"Just some drinks," I say. There's a flicker of worry before she resigns and leans in for a kiss. I tuck an errant strand of red hair behind her ear. "I'll call you later if you want."

"No, you have your night," she says. "I'll see you when you get home." She offers a smile. "Just drinking."

"That's it," I say.

"Okay, then."

We say I love you, then she's waving and shrinking in the side view as Quentin eases down the gravel drive. Julia and I are getting married in a week, which isn't ideal since we can't yet afford our own place. But that's the plan. Tonight's my stag, and Quentin, my best man, is in charge of the whole thing. I'm still on the fence, but I'm trying to be a good sport.

Once on the road, Quentin reaches behind my seat and hands me a can of Bud. "You ready, champ?"

"Ready as I'm gonna be."

"That's what I like to hear," he says, and guns the accelerator.

I crack the beer and drain half in one go. It's been a while since I've had one, and it tastes damn good. Quentin grabs himself a can, takes a long guzzle, burps, and lets out a satisfied *hoo-ee!* Then we ride in silence for a couple minutes out the pitted back roads toward his old man's place on Five Point Lake.

"So, what's the plan?" I say, and chuck my empty can out the window into the wind.

"Figure we'll take the boat out for a bit," he says. "Scoop up Jonesy on our way to the tittie bar."

"Anyone else?"

"Thought you said you wanted low key."

"I wasn't sure that phrase was in your vocab."

He laughs. "Well, we might run into an old friend or two."

This concerns me, if only because of what it implies.

"I'm not looking for any surprises," I say.

"Then you best not look in the glove box."

I look at him, but he doesn't take his eyes off the road. A grin plays at the corners of his mouth. After a beat, I reach for the dash and open the compartment to see about a quarter ounce of mushrooms in a Ziploc sitting atop the owner's manual. Quentin's grin is full blown now.

"Get the fuck outta here," I say.

#

Quentin's father owns several apartment complexes in and around the city and has his hands in a number of other things, including oil and gas. His house, which sits on a hill overlooking the lake, cost more than most people around here will see in their lifetimes. Just pulling up to the four-car garage is enough to put me on edge.

"Your old man home?"

"Out of town for the weekend," Quentin says.

"That's good," I say, and relax a little. It's not that the man is an outright prick, but he's got this leer that always puts me off. Most of the guys around these parts, myself included, come from long lines of mechanics and farmhands, waitresses and short order cooks. The kind of work where you get paid by the hour, or by the job, and lousy benefits mean you only go to the doctor if you think you're dying. And though Quentin's old man plays it nice enough, whenever I'm around he seems to engage me in the same conversation. *You working? Yeah, what they paying these days? Well, how about that.* Then he'll look around the room, pat a hand on one of his granite countertops and smile. Just enough to never quite know where I stand.

Fortunately Quentin didn't inherit this trait. His family circumstances keep him more than comfortable, but he's never rubbed anyone's nose in it, not once in the whole time I've known him. We met in high school, after he got kicked out of the military academy his folks had sent him to during their long and nasty divorce. Quentin was almost eighteen when he came home, so he finished out his last year at Middleton High. It was the only school in the township ever since the other ones closed back in the 70s, just before all the mills shut down and everything else in the Valley went to hell. He seemed better suited to the suburban crowd, but he knew how to party, and that was enough to rid most of us of our prejudices. We've been tight for nearly ten years, and even though we were out of touch for a while before Julia and I moved back up here to the boonies, it's one of the few bridges I've managed not to burn.

We go inside, grab a cooler from one of the closets, fill it with the rest of the case of Bud and a bottle of premixed Margarita, then head out back and down to the dock. The sunlight glitters on the calm water as I load the cooler into the long bowrider. Quentin unties us. I push us off and he fires up the engine.

"Toss me one of those brews," he says.

I toss him one, open another for myself, and we make waves toward the heart of the lake, while a blue heron cuts across the clear sky above us.

#

We tool around for a couple hours and head back just before the sun sinks behind the pines on the far bank. The beer and heat have gone to my head. My eyes are heavy, and I'm way too tired, so I stretch out on the sofa for a minute to rest my eyes. I hear Quentin go outside again, a car door open, then close.

"Look alive, champ," he says when he returns, tossing the bag of mushrooms at me. "We're just getting started."

"I've gotta pass a test," I say, sitting up and setting the bag on the coffee table.

"When?"

"Might be Monday, might be a week from now. They're random, that's how they get you. Got a warning last time. My third. One more and I'm done."

He considers this seriously for a minute. Then: "When have you ever known them to test for these?"

Now it's my turn to consider. He's got a point. If you've been around long enough, you know they only check for the big five, sometimes six. Fungus doesn't fit the bill, so I pick up the bag, unroll it. Could be bad news.

"Come on," Quentin says. "Down the hatch."

For a moment I see that look of worry flicker on Julia's face, and I'm almost ashamed at how easily I cast the thought aside. It takes me less than a minute to bounce between all the reasons why I should and why I shouldn't. Thoughts about what might happen. I reach in and pull one out, cap and stem still connected but not too big, then walk over to examine its blue streaks in the recessed lights above the mantle.

"Just this one," I say, turning to Quentin, telling myself it's a compromise. Loosen up and have some fun. You could use a little escape from reality. "And you're positive your old man's out of town?" I ask. "He's not gonna come strolling in just as the walls start breathing is he?"

"Like I told you," he says. "He's gone all weekend. And we'll be outta here before too long anyway. Now grow some balls."

Rather than search for flaws in his argument, I pop the mushroom in my mouth, chew it up, and wash it down with the last can of Bud. Let's see where this goes.

Afterward, we spend a little while getting ready. I don't own anything nicer than jeans and flannel shirts, but Quentin and I are the same size, so he loans me something to wear. We put on matching silk shirts and black jackets, mine offset with a slim red tie. It's as I'm standing in front of a hallway mirror, running a comb through my brown shag that I see the first shimmer, the first swell and stretch. Coming on like a spreading stain.

#

An hour later, we've hit the ATM and picked up Jonesy. He's wearing a similar outfit. We look like a jazz trio. A crew of card sharps. We're flying down the road at such high speed I'm thinking we might not see the sun come up. My molars are still mashed full of ground up mushroom and everything is trailing rainbows as the neon lights—cowboy boots and blinking spurs—break in the distance beyond the bridge.

Mustang Sally's sits on the far side of the Penn-Ohio truck stop, halfway between the city and the sticks. But despite the sign out front, it isn't all chaps and lassos. The roadhouse image long ago gave way to something more diverse. Now it's one of those joints where honky-tonk mixes with hip-hop and heavy metal. Where most of the girls are strung out on dope or crystal and wear caked-on make up to conceal their bruises. If you sit far enough back from the stage, you don't even notice the stretch marks and cesarean scars.

But that's on weekdays. Friday and Saturday nights are for the real talent. The hard bodies. The ones that draw a crowd. And tonight they're reeling in greasy cash from both ends of the county.

There's a line of sleazy freaks and wannabe ballers waiting to get in, but Quentin knows one of the owners, so he tucks a twenty in the doorman's pocket, and he waves us through. It's low lit inside, smoky. Off to the left, multicolored bottles of overpriced liquor stand lined up behind the bar. The surface of a long mirror that runs its length looks like water in a light breeze, wavy, reflecting the room back on itself in rippling curves. Makes the space seem bigger than it is.

Quentin's reserved an entire section for us. A petite girl in a leather corset, lacy boy-cut cheek huggers, and knee-high stilettos walks up and says, "Right this way, gentlemen," then ushers us over to an elevated part of the room closed off with velvet ropes, a section with a big table and cushioned seats.

"Tonight, it's all ours," Quentin shouts over the noise. He's grinning ear to ear and nodding his head. There's sweaty men reeking of cheap cologne crammed together at tiny tables, barely enough room for the cocktail waitresses to work their hustles, and here we are, just the three of us, lounging in a section big enough for a dozen or more. The rest of the guys in the place glare at us. I'm doing my best to soak it in. Cigars are passed around, tips are clipped. Someone lights mine and a drink appears before me. I sniff it: scotch, expensive. I've never felt so important in my entire life.

#

Lance, another one of my friends from way back shows up shortly after we do. He's not alone. Got some dude with him named Ramón, sporting head-to-toe Velour and a long tight braid. Lance looks the same as he always has. Shaved head, camo pants, and an oversized shirt with a dragon on it, like he just stepped out of high school. "What. Is. Up, man?" he says, slapping my hand and pulling me in for a one-arm hug. "Thought you were dead."

"Probably shoulda been," I say, and laugh despite the truth of it.

"Gettin' married," he says. "Goddamn."

For a minute we just stand around nodding and laughing. Awkward.

"Well, let's do this," he says. "My man's got a pocketful of tricks for the occasion."

I explain my situation, the drug test, and it's like I just told him I have inoperable cancer or something. He looks down at the floor and shakes his head in condolence. As if to say, *Tough break, man.*

"Gotta hit the head," I say, and make for the other side of the club. When I come out of the john, the four of them are doing shots at the bar. But there's this smog of desperation hanging in the place that's making it hard for me to enjoy myself, so when the girl I've been watching on stage approaches me after her set and leads me by the hand to the VIP room without a word, I'm glad to go.

There are those who really stand out, with their special acts, crafted and honed, who own the stage. Like the older one on the pole as we make our way through the private curtain, rattlesnake tattoo wrapped clear around her body, coiled and seeming to breathe beneath the flickering lights.

But this girl here, she reminds me of Julia more than a little. It's the first thing I noticed and the reason I've had my eye on her all night. Size-negative skinny with straight hair the color of red wine framing her made-up face.

Once, I asked Julia to strip for me before we made love. She seemed hesitant at first, but then she did. Even seemed to enjoy herself once she got going. "You know," she said, slowly peeling off her thin white tee, "maybe I should go do amateur night. I hear top vote gets like three hundred bucks, plus whatever you make dancing. Think I could win?" I did, and I told her so. At first, it was funny. Though now it's a memory I'd rather forget.

The girl bums a cigarette from me as we settle onto a purple couch, and she drapes her leg, slim and silky, over mine. The mild trip is past its peak, but everything still feels bent and unreal. My head is a whirling nebula. 80s hair metal comes through a surround sound system, distorted and strange. My head is supernova. A mirror ball throws fractured light that looks like screaming faces across the wall. My head is a neutron star.

She tells me anything goes, says, "It's all been taken care of." But by the time she almost burns me with her cigarette for the second time, it hits me how far gone she is. Her eyes were vacant as she danced on stage, tuned out, like she was really somewhere else, but now they're barely open. She's on the nod. A look I know too well. Julia and I have spent the last eight months in a methadone program over the state line in PA. Long drive every morning. It's kept us off the dope for a while now, but you never forget your own kind. They

264

tell their stories without even opening their mouths. It's all over their faces, in the scars on their arms, the regret they try to keep buried but which wells to the surface in just the right light. It's all there.

For the remainder of the hour, she leans against me while I give in to the overpowering urge to talk her ear off about anything and everything. About growing up not far from here. About dropping out of school to get a job. About moving around—Milwaukee, Oregon, Columbus, some smaller places in between—snowballing downhill from fun to fucked-up without seeing what was happening before it was too late. About getting clean—sort of. She sometimes mutters things as she nibbles on my ear, about her dreams, her plans, how she has it all figured out. She reaches between the buttons of my shirt and rubs my chest. Her hand is warm and soft. She whispers something low and breathy: maybe it's *Tell me what you like, baby* or *Do you want to fuck?* or *How do you want me?*

All I want is to tell her there are other options. But I don't. We remain on the couch, her half unconscious against me, me just wanting to be far from where I am. When the time is up, I wrap the rest of the bills Quentin gave me on our way into the club around a business card—my counselor's at the clinic—and place it in her palm, folding her fingers closed. "Take care," I whisper, and kiss her on the cheek. I hope she uses it, but she probably won't.

As she drifts back behind the scenes to get ready for another set, I realize that I never got her name, real or otherwise. And it's probably better that way.

265

#

The guys are all spread around throughout the club when I come out. Quentin and Lance are down front by the stage, throwing paper airplanes made out of dollar bills at the different dancers as they come and go. I can tell they're spun by the way their knees are bobbing, they way they keep rubbing their noses. I see Ramón hanging toward the back at a table with a girl on his lap. She's playing with his braid and giggling. Man with the goods. Leave it to Lance to know a guy like this. He always knows a guy. You need something, Lance will nine times out of ten know a guy. Drugs, custom car parts, a set of stereo speakers on the cheap—whatever it is, he'll make a phone call, maybe two, and find it for you. My freezer was once packed four sides deep with poached game—venison, rabbit, wild fucking boar—all because I made a passing comment about how I could go for some deer steak. Two days later, Lance showed up with a cooler full of packaged meat. No bullshit.

Up in our section, Jonesy sits at the table by himself, sipping on a bottle of Heineken and chewing on a fat cigar. When I sit down next to him he nods. He's never been much for talking. One of these stoic guys that likes to hang at the back of the group, eyes open and alert, but quiet, like the noise outside will never equal the noise inside. He's also a boxer. Quick. Agile. Cut up and lean. Moves around on legs like springs, always bouncing. More energy than he knows what to do with. It's as if his body and mind belong to separate people, one calm and reserved, the other high strung and ready to scrap. Put some speed in front of him, you've

266

got a time bomb. And it's looking to me now like he's about to blow his lid.

"What's itchin' you, Jonesy?"

"Fat motherfucker keeps eyein' us."

"What? Who?" I look around. Down by the stage, closer to us than Lance and Quentin, I catch some heavyset guy in a leather jacket glance our way.

"Been mean muggin' us since we walked in," Jonesy says.

"What's he gonna do?" I say. "There's four of us, five if you count Lance's boy."

"Don't need to be but one of us," he says, and that's when I know we need to get out of here.

"Fuck that guy," I say. "I want to split, anyway." I smack him on the back. "I'm gonna go round up the others."

"So'd you get it wet?" Quentin asks when I get to where they're sitting.

"I think we oughta roll out," I say. "Move this someplace else."

"Already? Why?"

"I'm over it. And I think Jonesy's about to unwind on some dude."

They both follow my nod toward our table, but there's no one there. My eyes trace a line toward the other side of the stage, where Jonesy's closing in on the guy. "Oh, shit."

267

There's just enough time for me to say it again before they see what I see.

Jonesy shoves the guy. The music is too loud to hear his voice, but his mouth makes all the shapes of *You got a fuckin' problem, motherfucker?* Dude gets up from his chair, but before he's even standing, Jonesy lights him up with three punches, maybe more. The guy stumbles back but doesn't go down. Heads turn as another set of blows puts him over a table and sends glasses crashing to the floor.

This time the three of us say it together: "Oh, shit."

We move, rush over and grab Jonesy. People love a good fight, hate when it ends too soon. Shouts and cheers follow us toward the door, out the door. I thought the trip was over, but I feel fingers in my brain, and suddenly it's like I'm in a twisted circus show. Our group has grown. *Wait, who the fuck is this now?* I'm in an SUV surrounded by clowns. They're hanging out the windows, cackling and whooping as we streak down the road behind Lance and Ramón, barreling through the night toward who knows where.

Ramón's got a house not far from where I lived for about a year when I was a kid. Over on the East Side. A mostly broken-down neighborhood of boxy bungalows that slopes into the scraped out Valley like it's about to topple over. Dude knows how to keep things low profile. The outside of his place is about as unassuming as it gets. Not extravagant, not shabby, but just the right amount of well-kept: fenced-in yard, porch swing, light blue paint and dark blue shutters, flowerbeds, the whole nine. Like an old lady lives here. I'm thinking he must live with his grandma, maybe an old aunt or something, but when we walk in, I see it's all for show.

The kitchen is dark hardwood and track lighting, chrome appliances and stone tile. Living room floored with colorful rugs. A fireplace. There's an aquarium full of exotic fish built into one wall, a stocked bar in the corner, and an array of couches and chairs that look like clouds. Ramón tells us to make ourselves comfortable and vanishes into a back room with one of the tag-along girls from the club. Quentin fills rocks glasses decked in dollar signs with vodka, rum, gin and tonic, passes them around. My mouth is so dry I can't even taste what I'm drinking.

Lance is already on his phone, pacing from room to room, casting his net. Minutes later he kicks back with his drink in a cushy lounge chair and says, "Party's on its way."

"On its way," I echo, and we clank glasses.

I consider ducking into the bathroom to call Julia, but then it's in front of me. The crystal. The pills. For the first time tonight, laid out on the table. It was only a matter of time. The fierce quickness with which I disregard everything. No one even questions my sudden change of heart.

Another twenty minutes pass, thirty, forty-five, I don't really know because whenever I check my phone or a clock the numbers start moving around on me. But it's like I blink and I blink and at one point I blink again and the amount of people has doubled, then tripled. All blurs. Moving bodies, voices talking in circles.

Quentin and some guy I've never met are jabbering on and on to each other about things I can't quite decipher. Cars or politics. Lance has his phone wedged between his ear and shoulder, a Newport clamped in his teeth, talking, and squinting through the smoke while he plays an Xbox game. Others—guys, girls—are spread about on couches and chairs, hanging out, making out, passed out cold.

My body feels like an exposed nerve ending. I get up from the couch where I've been sitting for maybe minutes or maybe hours and ask Ramón, "You got somewhere I can chill out by myself for a minute?"

He nods like he gets it, says, "I got you." I follow him into the finished basement where there's a separate, smaller party going on. Beneath a window on the far side of the room, Jonesy grunts and boxes with his shadow. Ramón waves me forward. There's a small room off the main space, in the process of being remodeled: fresh drywall, some stacks of boxes and a twin mattress on the floor.

"You like toys?" he asks me, and for a few seconds I think dude's going funny on me. Then he opens one of the boxes on the floor and reaches in, pulls out some G.I. Joe action figures and hands them to me. I don't know what I was expecting, but it sure wasn't this. I lean over and look into the box. It's filled with toys. Transformers and Thundercats and Teenage Mutant Ninja Turtles. He-Man and the Masters of the Universe. Mr. Potato Head, matchbox cars, an Etch-a-Sketch. More stuff buried beneath it all. My entire childhood in a box. I look up at Ramón and must be smiling because he says, "Go on, playa,' take a walk down memory lane. Ain't no one gonna bother you in here."

He leaves, goes back out into the blur, and I'm alone for the first time tonight, not alone in a room full of people, but really alone, listening to them all out there and above me. It's still hard to say where the time is or where it's going, but as I explore the box in the corner, digging deeper and deeper, it doesn't much seem to matter.

We drop off Jonesy first since I'm the farthest out, and by the time Quentin turns off Route 67 into Julia's folks' driveway, it's after 5:00 but still full dark, that time of morning when the birds haven't yet started singing and it's hard to decide whether it's early or late, today or still the day before. His headlights sweep through the morning fog, casting tree shadows on the side of the house, which sits back about quarter mile from the road. The sound of crunching gravel, of weeds from the rutted driveway flicking at the bottom of the truck, the whisper of the waist-high corn through our open windows—it all seems especially loud in the stillness of the hour.

We moved back here from the city last winter when things got bad and we couldn't pay our rent anymore. I hadn't heard from my folks since they wrote me off in a letter the year before, and we had nowhere else to turn. It was the usual plan, simple as it sounds: wrestle the old cold turkey,

271

get some fresh country air, and get our heads together. Then, somewhere along the way, we decided we should get married.

But simple gets confused with easy by smarter people than me.

Since being in the clinic, we've been okay. Mostly. But lately, I've been lamenting the good times, hard as they are to recall most days. The methadone keeps us well, but crutches alone don't mend broken bones, and there's always something else to lean on. As far as truth goes, Julia knows I've slipped up a few times, but she's got no idea I'm about to get kicked out of the program if I piss dirty one more time. She's embraced what, for her, is a second chance. But for me—shit, I've lost count. It really is a miracle we've made it this far.

Quentin circles the turnaround and lets me out.

"If Julia asks," he says, "go easy on the details."

"Just a casual night with the guys," I say. We grin at each other, and although I spent most of the night wishing I'd just stayed home, I say, "Thanks, Quent, for everything. I mean it."

"What's a best man for?" He winks.

I tap the quarter panel and tell him to split before someone wakes up.

"Roger that," he says.

For a moment I stand watching him leave, taillights fading in a cloud of dust, and I know that what we have just can't last.

Inside, the house is quiet. Everyone's still asleep and will be for at least a couple hours. The clinic is closed on the weekends, and my skin is beginning to tingle in a bad way, so I drink my take-home dose, then sneak into our room, slip out of my clothes and into bed. Julia's lying on her side beneath a thin sheet. I stretch out on my back and listen to her shallow breaths for a while, a peaceful sound, and watch as the edges of her body grow sharper in the rising light outside the window.

But as tired as I am, sleep is still far off.

I get up and creep back into the hall. Julia's folks are snoring, the call and response of two congested birds, but still I tip-toe past their door.

The crawl space is in an alcove at the top of the stairs, and that's where I seek the place I need. I waddle in on my haunches, pick up the flashlight that sits just inside, kept here since there is no light, and pull the small door closed behind me. It doesn't take me long to find what I'm looking for. The box is toward the back wall, under a pile of old quilts and moth-eaten linens. The box of junk from my childhood, things it's a wonder I haven't lost over the years.

I pull out action figures, Happy Meal toys, and other relics. I set them all around me on the dusty wooden floor. With Legos I try to build a wall around myself, but there

273

aren't nearly enough, so I use boxes and bins and whatever else I can find, cover it all with a quilt and climb inside.

Soon, they'll all be awake. Soon, sometime today or tomorrow, Julia's family will begin arriving from out of town. Aunts and uncles, cousins and grandparents from all over. They'll be staying the week, filling the spare rooms and sleeping on couches until after the wedding.

I hear that word. Wedding. It tolls in my skull like an ominous bell.

Soon there will be a wedding.

A rehearsal dinner.

A ceremony and a reception.

There are just so many things they do not know, these people, and I wonder how much pressure it will take to crack. For this wall to finally crumble. But there's no way of knowing just now, here in this musty space. Here, where it's just me and these remaining bits of who I was, holding on.

Acknowledgments

Many thanks are owed to the editors of the following publications, in which several of these stories first appeared in slightly different form: "Trapper's Creek" was published in *Elm Leaves Journal*; "Something Special" and "The Call" were published in *Floyd County Moonshine*; "Letting Go" was published in *All We Need of Hell*, the special Harry Crews tribute issue of *Cowboy Jamboree*; "Portraits of the Dead and Dying" and "Running" were published in *Literally Stories*; "The Thirteenth Step" was published in *New World Writing*; "Talking and Standing Still" was published in *The Vignette Review*; and "The Bad Ones" was published in *The Fictioneer*.

As for others, I couldn't have written these stories if it were not for the guidance and support of a number of people: first, my friend and mentor Christopher Barzak, for your faith and encouragement from the start, and for opening a whole new world to me with your first book recommendations—you know the ones; Steven Reese, Colleen Clayton, Mindi Kirchner-Greenway, Teresa Leone, Rebecca Barnhouse, Eric Wasserman, Varley O'Conner, and Robert Miltner, for your guidance and enthusiasm along the way; and all of my friends and colleagues at Youngstown State University and in the NEOMFA program. I wouldn't be where I am without you.

Many thanks go to Brian Evenson and Mitchell S. Jackson, both of whom I had the great privilege of working with during my stay at the Juniper Writing Institute and who opened my eyes to many things in such a short time. The Juniper Crew and Friends of Tina's Titties—you all kick infinite ass, and I'm glad to have you in my circle. Rusty Barnes, I can't thank you enough for your friendship, support, and massive talent. And of course, Kim Chinquee and Tamara Grisanti, I'll never forget your generosity and kind words.

Endless gratitude to Summer Stewart, Caitlin James, and the great folks over at Unsolicited Press for taking on this project and for their hard work.

Thanks also to all the writers whose work has been a continual source of inspiration for me, who have helped me see that there's no shortage of stories to be told and that it's often the small moments that carry the most weight.

I'd like to further extend my gratitude to my city, Youngstown, OH. You don't get enough love, but you've got mine. Also, a nod to the small, outlying rural communities, where I spent many years of my youth and which served as models for me while I was creating the town of Miles Junction, which, though an amalgam of real places, is purely fictional. The countless characters I've known in these places, good and bad and worse, a nod to you, as well.

Thank you to my mother, for always seeing that I had food, clothes, shelter, and love. No matter what. And thank you to the rest of my family, near and far, for whatever parts you play in my story.

Finally, my wife, Rebecca, and my children, Spencer and Esmé—thank you for giving me a reason to wake up each day, a reason to keep going, to keep trying. I love you.

About the Author

William R. Soldan grew up in and around Youngstown, Ohio, with brief stints in Columbus; Milwaukee, Wisconsin; and the hills of southern Oregon. When he was seventeen, he dropped out of high school at the suggestion of his guidance counselor and worked a long string of jobs including factory machinist, dishwasher, house painter, maintenance man, day laborer, and bartender. After traveling around and living out of a van for a while, he eventually went to college and earned a BA in Literature from Youngstown State University and an MFA from the Northeast Ohio Master of Fine Arts program. Nominated for a Pushcart Prize multiple times, his work has appeared in numerous journals and anthologies such as *New World Writing, Elm Leaves Journal, Cowboy Jamboree, Kentucky Review, Jelly Bucket, Tough, The Best American Mystery Stories* 2017, and others. He currently resides in Youngstown with his wife and two children.

About the Press

Unsolicited Press was founded in 2012 and is currently based in Portland, Oregon. The volunteer-based press publishes exemplary fiction, creative nonfiction, and poetry from award-winning authors.

Learn more at www.unsolicitedpress.com.